To: Leanne

Thanks for being a reader !!
Enjoy and feel free to share.
Jah Bless !!

8/25/15

THE GENESIS
(Back 2 My Rootz Vol. 1)

Also by Peprah Boasiako:

THE HITMAN: A Short Story
THE SEXTAPE: A Dedication to the Ladies

Upcoming projects by Peprah Boasiako:

Lost Cause
Latoya 1 & 2
Feel My Pain
The Stepchild

For more information, visit the author's website at:

www.peprahboasiako.com

THE GENESIS
(Back 2 My Rootz Vol. 1)

PEPRAH BOASIAKO

Ground-Up Media

Bronx, New York

Ground-Up Media
951 Hoe Avenue, 7G
Bronx, New York 10459
(347) 912-1323
GUMpublishing@gmail.com
www.peprahboasiako.com

****

****

Cover Design: Kim Black of TOJ Publishing Services

First Ground-Up Media trade paperback edition 2015

Library of Congress Control Number: 2015909055

ISBN: 9781942845041 (Pbk)

ISBN: 9781942845447 (Hbk)

For information about special discounts for bulk purchases, please contact Ground-Up Media sales at:

(347) 912-1323 or GUMpublishing@gmail.com

10 9 8 7 6 5 4 3 2 1

Printed in the United States of America

DEDICATION

IN LOVING MEMORY OF A FALLEN COMRADE-IN-ARMS, JEFF LEBRUN (1983 – 2005)

"The Beautiful Struggle."

ACKNOWLEDGEMENTS

I'd like to thank the man above without whom none of this would be possible.

To my family, thank you for standing by me.

To Antoine, Kwesi and Patrick, may the memories never fade!

Special thanks to Jennifer, for her contribution to this beautiful cover.

To my designer, Kim, thanks for blessing a brother with those awesome covers.

To anybody I didn't mention, please don't take it personal.

THE GENESIS
BACK 2 MY ROOTZ VOL. 1

PROLOGUE

Darkness gradually looms over the fall skies on the evening of KD's last night in New York. Tonight, he leaves for a very special vacation. An untimely but much needed vacation, possibly with no return. *No one knows what the future holds,* they say. But how does one explain this sudden change?

Is my life some kind of movie script, with edits at any possible moment? What bothers me most is that I'm not the one making the edits. KD's thoughts run rampant as he stares blankly out of the sliding glass doors leading to the patio.

This is the life I chose, the path I've travelled on, and well, tonight, I must continue my journey. He concludes to himself quietly.

Never let them see you sweat. His uncle Black always said to him as he was growing up. Tonight, he's no longer that teenage boy, with his manhood put to the ultimate test as he faces this untimely challenge. Will he pass or will he fail? Only time will tell.

In a matter of hours, the place he's called home for nearly three decades would become a mere blurry sight, as he travels back to his roots. The place he has lived and loved his entire adult life, forging unbreakable relationships with some of the most beautiful and important individuals he's ever encountered. How does one cope with such a major change? Bad enough most people think he's been dead.

Sitting in the spacious living room of Black's house in Jersey, surrounded by custom-made furniture, expensive pieces of art and fancy electronics, he thinks about what life would be like back across the ocean after such a lengthy absence. From the plush crème leather sofa where he sits, the balls of his heels sink deep into the matching crème-colored carpet as he stares absentmindedly at a portrait of Bob Marley, the late great reggae legend. In this particular portrait, the legend appears to be in deep thought, similar to the position KD finds himself in now. This makes him wonder just what was going through Mr. Marley's mind at that particular point in time.

The spliff he clutched between the middle and index fingers of his left hand burns freely; traces of smoke rising towards the spinning ceiling fan as he continues to stare at the portrait, reminiscing about his life here in New York. The life that would soon become his past, part of his history. He remembers all the fun times he shared with his *brothers*, Dolla and Poundz, as well as the bad times. The near death situations, especially the incident that prompted Black to draw the conclusion to let the wrong right itself.

Having jumped bail on a double homicide, the authorities sought after him heavily. The hefty bounty Nine placed on his head for the death of Dre didn't make matters any easier. Hell, with a bounty that healthy, your own mama would start to look like the threat. Black's suggestion that KD take an overdue vacation until things blow over seems reasonable at this point. After all, he no longer exists to most people, so why not confirm their suspicions?

Granted this is a smart idea, the fact that his *brothers*, like most people, think he's dead does not appeal to him. In fact, it burns deeply inside him day in and out. Considering everything they've been through together, no one deserves to know he is alive more than Dolla and Poundz, his *brothers* from another mother. For it's because of his *death* that Dolla and Poundz have been mercilessly warring with Nine over the last few months. Word on the streets is that they swore they wouldn't rest until Nine is dead and gone.

This bloodshed has got to stop! He says to myself as he finishes his spliff and tosses the roach into the glass ashtray. As far as he could see, he is the key to this complicated puzzle — Nine wants to kill him to avenge Dre's death, and his *brothers* want Nine dead because they think he's responsible for the incident that *killed* Black and him. Talk about a touchy situation.

I need to do something before someone else gets hurt, or worse, ends up dead. He says to himself.

With that thought in mind, he downs the glass of Hennessy he's been babysitting and slips into his Timberland boots. Snatching his .45 from the coffee table, he tucks the gun into his waistline and without wasting another minute, heads out into the darkness. In the garage, he occupies the driver's seat of Black's Chrysler 300. He stashes the pistol under his seat before turning the engine over. As the engine purrs quietly, he thinks shortly about what he is doing.

Since the only way to stop the bloody war is by showing his brothers that he is still alive, he presses the button to open the garage door and watches through the rearview mirror as it retreats upward. Before the door could fully clear, he reverses out of the garage on his way to pay his *brothers* a surprise visit.

The silence in the car is deafening as he maneuvers his way towards the George Washington Bridge. He makes it to the bridge quickly and stays the course into New York, driving at a normal speed to help collect his thoughts. Once in New York, he tunes the car's satellite radio to an R&B station, keeping the volume just above a whisper, thankful for light traffic.

Past the tollbooths with no hassle, he realizes just a few blocks away from Dolla's house that he's been driving longer than an hour. He continues to navigate his way through the back streets until he arrives at Dolla's address. To be on the safe side, he decides to drive around the neighborhood to get a feel for the area. Considering how secluded the neighborhood is, he finds little activity as expected.

On his second go-around, he eases the 300 to the curbside up the street from Dolla's house. Cutting off the lights, he lets the engine idle for a moment. He transfers his .45 to his waist and quickly scans the street before killing the engine and making his exit. No sooner than his Timberlands make contact with the pavement, a burst of gunfire erupts from the direction of Dolla's house. Caught completely off guard, he quickly ducks behind the car, removing his own pistol from his waistline. On his haunches, he scans the street again, not a soul is in sight.

The gunfire continues; an exchange from what sounded like three different guns. An obvious firefight in his *brother's* house drives his heart to beat as loud as an African drum. He waits during a moment of cease-fire, followed by two distinct shots, then a long silence. A lump forms in his throat. An ordeal lasting a minute or two feels like hours to him. He says a quick prayer, asking God to spare his *brothers'* lives.

Fueled by adrenaline, he snaps into action. After another quick scan of the street before advancing cautiously towards the front of Dolla's house, he could see the front door cracked open as he approaches.

"This can't be good," he whispers over his loud heartbeats.

He creeps up and cautiously enters the house, gun at the ready. Bingo! Lifeless bodies lay sprawled on the floor just as he expects; two in the kitchen and a third in the living room. He's overflowing with adrenaline by now. A quick examination of the bodies reveals two strangers and one familiar face. He sees broken glass and blood every step he takes.

Where the fuck is Dolla and Poundz? He wonders. He proceeds cautiously but effectively to check the rest of the house. As he steps out of the kitchen area and into the hallway, he hears faint voices from down the hall. Although he's not making out exactly the conversation, he pinpoints two distinct voices. He advances carefully in the direction of the voices, gun still at the ready. Halfway down the hall, he makes out some of the words mentioned — something about last words or last wishes. He continues to inch closer and closer until he is mere feet from a half-opened bedroom door.

From this position, he doesn't have a clear view of the room but he distinctly hears the conversation.

"You die tonight, muthafucka!" A male voice bellows.

"Fuck you, pussy!" Spouts from another.

This second voice sounds like Dolla, which prompts KD to lean in closer for a better look. He leans in just in time to see an unfamiliar man strike a kneeling Dolla in the back of the head with a pistol. Dolla screams out in pain, holding his head, then follows with, "Eat a dick, Nine!"

"Nine?" He whispers to himself. He is so furious that he follows his anger, barging into the room with such quickness that neither man acknowledges his presence.

"Die, mutha..." Is the last thing he hears Nine say before he silences him mid-sentence with a headshot from his .45.

Nine drops next to Dolla with a loud thud. For emphasis, he pumps two more shots into Nine's back as he lays slump on the floor. Not a pretty sight. He takes a moment to examine the rest of the room — no other threats. He considers checking the rest of the house for threats but he also understands that time isn't on his side.

No time for small talk, he could hear the wailing of sirens from afar. From around his neck, he removes his African necklace, the one with the Rastafarian colors, and places it atop Nine's lifeless body. Without a word, he runs out of the room, leaving a still-kneeling Dolla in shock. He sprints back to the 300, pistol still in hand. He quickly takes the driver's seat, turns the engine over, and pulls off the curb, leaving a trail of black rubber on the asphalt.

A couple of left and right turns later, he is relieved to finally be out of the area. He takes the drive back to

Jersey in complete silence. However, don't let me get too far ahead. Good storytellers tell their stories from the beginning. Let's start from the top, where it all began.

Chapter 1: THE GENESIS

The year was 1989. King "KD" Diamond was just an innocent young boy, five years old to be exact. He didn't know much about the world or many of the things in it, for that matter. Though he had just migrated to America, he was far from your average five-year-old boy. At this age, KD had experienced more than most people would in their lifetime.

At the tender age of three, he lost his entire immediate family to a house fire. Out of his five-member family, he emerged as the sole survivor. Trapped in their burning house, his mother, father, and two older siblings hadn't been so lucky, dying from numerous internal and external injuries. KD managed to cheat death but that didn't go without saying he suffered serious injuries all over the lower half of his body. For years following this incident, KD suffered nightmares night after night.

With his family gone, the responsibility fell on his maternal grandmother, Cici, to care for him. Cici, having raised six children of her own, hadn't backed down. She stepped right up to the plate, adopting KD and caring for him until he was fully well again.

Having no other choice, KD learned to adapt to growing up with Cici. Over the years, Cici tried her hardest to conceal from KD the facts of his family's disappearance, mostly due to his age at the time. He possessed this persistent *I need to know* force within him, however, that drove Cici crazy.

Finally, Cici gave in, gradually telling KD bits and pieces of the story as time went on. The unbelievable story of how his alcoholic father, during one of his drunken rages, had started a fight with his mother and had decided to set their house on fire in an attempt to wipe them all out. This disturbing story became more of a bedtime story for KD. No matter how far-fetched it sounded at first, after hearing it over and over, he believed that was how he lost his family and continued to do so through his adult years.

During his time at Cici's house, KD also learned of the man known as Black, after constantly nagging at his grandmother day in and out about the photographs that hung on her living room walls. Guess he was just a curious kid, and who could blame him?

"That's your uncle Kwesi and his family. You'll get to meet them one day." Cici calmly told him day after day.

Of course, he wouldn't end it there. "Who is that little boy? Where do they live? Why are they dressed like that?" KD's questions ran endless!

Yet, poor Cici took her time to answer every single one. After a while, it became more of a pastime for the two of them. After dinner, the two would sit on the veranda in front of the house and chat about any and everything. In Cici's eyes, KD was a special child, maybe even the most special of all her grandchildren.

$$$$$

Kwesi "Black" Blackman, the man who brought KD to America, was far from average. As tough as a nail, Black was a legend in underground operations with a certified track record. An alien maternal uncle of KD's, the only thing KD knew of this man was the many photographs that hung inside his grandmother's house and the stories his grandmother told him. Stories about how Black had left for America during his early twenties, establishing a family there and only returning home for short visits every so often.

Over time, KD understood why he never knew much of him. With a wife and a son of his own living in New York City, along with a number of businesses that he operated, it made sense that Black only visited home every few years.

Unfortunately for KD, he never had the opportunity to meet his cousin or aunt. In the months leading to his migration to the United States, tragedy struck Black's family. Black lost his lovely wife and only child to a horrible car accident, involving a drunk motorcyclist — Black's wife and their six-year-old son pronounced dead on the scene.

Arrested and jailed, the drunk cyclist never saw his day in court. The justice system's slow and lengthy trial process hadn't been enough to satisfy Black. In fact, it led Black to take action, getting the drunk bastard murdered right in his jail cell.

Following this, Black travelled back home to seek clarity. He spent a total of three months clearing his head. During this time, Cici convinced him to take KD with him abroad. Black had been reluctant at first but considering the circumstances, he had given in.

So, here KD was, on that faithful spring day in 1989, a five-year-old boy, travelling to America for the first time. With his dead cousin's passport, he had no problem entering New York City. And that was the beginning of his *American dream*.

Chapter 2: A HAPPY HOME

Upon arriving at America, Black brought KD to his home, or what KD thought was his home. There, he introduced him to a lady, whom KD took to be Black's girlfriend. This lovely Jamaican lady whom KD came to know as Ms. Gladys became the best mom any five-year-old boy could ask for. For a childless woman, Ms. Gladys spoiled KD with unconditional love. She treated KD as if he was her own.

In New York City, Grant Avenue and 165th Street in the Bronx served as his first home. Hmmm! The unforgettable memories he'd shared with Ms. Gladys in that third floor apartment. One could never forget climbing the stairs of 1007 to the third floor multiple times on a daily basis. But hey, that was how it was when your building had no elevator. You humped it out every day with the groceries, the laundry, and everything else because life must go on.

Ms. Gladys, whom KD later discovered was Black's main girlfriend, took KD in and cared for him as if he was her own. When he felt sick, as a nurse herself, she was there by his side. The two of them became well known at the emergency room of Lincoln Hospital.

Despite the gifts and affection she spoiled KD with Ms. Gladys had no problem whipping his behind when he behaved badly. She believed in the saying, 'spare the rod, you spoil the child.' One time, she whipped him so hard for disrespecting a lady in the streets, KD was scared to sit on his butt afterwards.

Being the little boy that KD was, he never understood many things here in America. First, it was the snow and the cold weather he had to adapt to, an adjustment that took him years to accomplish. Then, the different mix of people, the way people dressed, the different foods, languages and sports — the American way of life as they called it.

On top of it all, KD never understood why they called him a different name at school. It just didn't make sense to him. At home, they'd call him by his nickname, KD, but then once he was at school, it was a very different story. No one seemed to call him by the name given by his parents. This just led KD to think that America was just one weird place!

Ms. Gladys made it her duty to make sure KD never wanted for anything. She made sure he was comfortable and that he got to school on time every day. KD's most distinctive memory — when he turned six. Ms. Gladys organized the first birthday party of his life.

Chapter 3: LA FAMILIA

Growing up in the hood, KD always heard the phrase, *ain't no friends in this game*, but he never really understood what it meant. The choices he made and the path he chose to travel upon later down the line helped him interpret this phrase. Over time, the phrase embedded in his brain. As a young man now, he grew to recognize the very truth to it, the reason he only surrounded himself with *family*.

In KD's world, someone was either with him or against him, no room for half-steppers. His *family* was built upon these values: a tight-knit family bound by a common goal in life — strive to achieve success in the drug game no matter the cost. With his two *brothers* at his side, and a backing from his Uncle Black, KD was unstoppable. His family consisted of an inseparable group of young and reckless individuals, with a huge appetite for success. When it came to their quest in the streets, these three would stop at nothing until they got results.

Juan "Dolla" Sanchez and Roberto "Poundz" Sanchez were blood brothers of Hispanic descent, whom KD had met in his neighborhood upon his migration to New York City. Living in the same apartment building and attending the same public schools, the three had quickly taken a liking to one another. They'd walk or ride to school and engage in after-school activities together, forming an unbreakable bond amongst themselves. Betting on pick-up basketball games around their neighborhood was their pastime, which only strengthened their bond over time.

While Dolla and KD were the same age, Poundz was only a year behind them, making him the baby of their family. With their unique individual styles and qualities, they complimented each other very well, and collectively, their strength exceeded that of a wolf pack. From the outside looking in, one would think the three were blood relatives from the way they stuck together, as well as stuck up for one another.

Dolla, with his superb mental capabilities, was the brain of their family. Wearing his hair in a low Caesar since a young boy, Dolla was a true thinker, and a clever one. He would orchestrate and collectively, they'd execute the wildest schemes in their times of need. At about five-foot-nine-inches and one-hundred-and-seventy-five-pounds soaking wet, Dolla was the smallest member of their family. Always calm and collective, one never knew what Dolla was thinking. "Never let your left hand know what your right hand is thinking." He always said through the years.

Poundz, on the other hand, was the pretty boy player type. Wearing his hair in cornrows since a baby, he had a razor-sharp tongue that got him into places he was not expected to be seen. At a lanky six-five and one-ninety, Poundz was the tallest member of their family and a natural on the basketball court. Contrary to his basketball talent, however, he'd mastered the art of slick talk. Poundz was definitely the type of cat you wouldn't want to leave your girl around. In the hood, he was reputed for bedding different girls and having them splurge on him. To be fair, Poundz could talk a new mother right out of her baby's diaper money.

Then there was KD, the muscle of their family. A tar-black, wide-bodied, dreadlock-wearing, cold bastard and he loved every bit of it. With multi-colored legs due to a childhood injury, KD was not to be fucked with. Standing at six-foot-three-inches and two-hundred-and-fifteen-pounds with the build of an NFL linebacker, KD's presence alone intimidated others. Cats in the hood knew playing with KD the wrong way came with consequences. This was mainly due to the numerous examples he'd made out of those who'd stepped on his toes in the past.

From the very beginning, on Grant Avenue, to the halls of Taft High, where they had all graduated from, it had been one for all and all for one. To say that they loved each other would be an understatement. Like most young people, their high school days were the wildest. One incident in particular solidified their brotherhood.

KD and Dolla were eleventh-graders, and Poundz, a tenth-grader at William Taft High School in the Bronx. KD, doing what he did best during a boring class, decided to waste time in the bathroom. Obtaining a hall-pass, he'd taken his sweet time getting to the bathroom since he didn't really need to go. This was a routine for him.

As he entered the bathroom, he heard commotion from the back of the room. *What's going on in here?* He thought to himself. He walked carefully inside, where he saw a Poundz look-alike being jumped by two Hispanic kids. The Poundz look-alike, who happened to be on the bottom of the pile, fought back with all his might, but was just overpowered by the other kids.

"What the fuck?" He mumbled more to himself as he tried to get a good look at the kid in trouble.

He only needed to see one thing: the red plaid shirt Poundz was wearing when they walked to school that morning. His energy similar to that of a raging bull, he grabbed the first Hispanic kid by his shirt and left shoulder, and flung him into the bathroom wall, leaving him dazed. The second Hispanic kid had long hair so he grabbed a handful and yanked his head back. The pain took his attention off Poundz as he attempted to pry KD's hand away. Poundz delivered a kidney shot with his left fist before KD freed the kid's hair.

Before KD realized, Poundz sat on top of the Hispanic kid, hitting him with endless blows. KD turned his back just in time to see the kid he had flung into the wall bull-rushing him. Unable to move out of the way quickly enough, he slammed into the wall hard. Now he felt dazed. The kid hit him with a one-two combo, which woke him right back up.

He blocked the next blow and countered with one of his own to the gut. A whimper escaped from the kid's mouth but that didn't stop KD.

KD followed with a weak kick to the kid's rib, curtesy of his soccer skills. That kick didn't do much damage because the kid came right back with a haymaker. KD sidestepped the blow and bull-rushed the kid, slamming him hard against the wall. Grabbing the kid by his shirt, KD delivered a head-butt that sent the kid straight to the floor. Adrenalin turned him into a monster, like the Incredible Hulk.

He took a quick look over his shoulder and saw Poundz still going to work on the other kid. As a final act of disrespect, KD walked over and slapped his opponent open-handedly across the face. The kid whimpered again, and it was obvious he didn't have much fight left in him.

KD then walked over and pulled Poundz off his opponent saying, "That's enough, son; that's enough!"

Poundz spat on his opponent as he and KD got

ready to leave the bathroom, struggling to catch their breaths. Before they made their way outside of the bathroom, however, they heard, "This shit ain't over, putas!"

Ignoring the kid's whining, Poundz said with conviction, "Good looking, son! We gonna finish these clowns later."

The two split, exiting the bathroom one after the other and going their separate ways. KD returned to class, doing his best to hide the stress on his face. Of course, they didn't get away with it. KD was called to the principal's office within the hour, where Poundz awaited with a small bruise on his left cheek. The principal also called the two Hispanic kids, one of whom had a bloody nose and the other, a busted lip.

When questioned about the bathroom incident, though, KD played the innocent passerby role. Regardless of the Hispanic kids' insistence that he partook in the brawl, he stuck to his story of being nothing other than a passerby. Poundz supported KD's story, claiming he was the victim of an attack by the Hispanic kids. Talks of suspensions for the four of them were in the air and phone calls were placed to their respective parents.

When the smoke cleared, however, the principal pardoned KD. Since there were no visible cuts or bruises on his body, or nothing to indicate that he was in fact part of the brawl, the principal couldn't punish him based solely on accusations.

During their routine after-school spliff session back on their block, Poundz revealed the actual cause of that brawl. Apparently, Poundz got head from one of the Hispanic kids' girlfriend, and started a rumor about her. To add insult to injury, when the kid confronted Poundz in the bathroom, Poundz gave the kid some hurtful details as well as labeled his girlfriend a slut. They had a good laugh during that afternoon's smoking session. While Poundz was clearly in the wrong in this particular situation, family was family and whether right or wrong, they always held each other down!

Chapter 4: MURDER SHE WROTE

Andre "Dre" Jackson wasn't just a regular worm trying to find his place inside the Big Apple. Dre's upbringing had not been as pleasant as most of his peers, and to say that he had a fucked up childhood would be a mere understatement. For starters, Dre lost his father to a heroin overdose as an infant. After his father's death, Comfort Jackson, his God-fearing mother juggled two jobs to support Dre and his older brother, Nine. Destiny soon interfered, however, claiming Comfort's poor soul soon after Dre's sixth birthday.

Rumor had it that Comfort caught wind of her new husband Charlie's extra marital activities. When she confronted him, Charlie hadn't been so receptive. His response had been, "Bitch, I'm a man, I come home when I want to." An argument ensued, leading to a physical fight and ultimately, Comfort's unfortunate death. To add insult to injury, the state prosecutor only agreed to an eight-year manslaughter sentence for Charlie, calling Comfort's untimely demise *accidental*.

Following this incident, Dre and Nine despised Charlie and everything he stood for. Nine, the older of the two, swore to avenge their mother's death no matter the cost. For countless nights, when a young Dre would wake up, crying for his mother, Nine held and comforted him, whispering, "Is gonna be alright. I'mma get him, I promise, I'mma get him for mommy." Nine would repeat this phrase until Dre returned to sleep.

It was no surprise when Nine gunned Charlie down in broad daylight soon after he was released from prison. Nine, barely eighteen at the time, was arrested, charged, convicted at trial, and sentenced to a prison term for Charlie's murder. The prosecutor's belief that Nine sought revenge for his mother's death resulted in a conviction for pre-meditated murder, resulting in a life sentence and leaving a fourteen-year-old Dre an emotional wreck.

With Nine gone to prison, Dre gradually became violent, often lashing out over petty things. For his violent behaviors, among other things, Dre was suspended from school for some time. During his suspension, Dre told himself, *Fuck school, and fuck the world as a whole.* To him, nobody gave a fuck. Dre went on to replace his foster parents with the streets on a quest for peace. He didn't see a future in staying with his foster parents, and so he made the decision to find himself another home. He needed a place where he could feel at peace.

Now a run-away, Dre boosted, robbed and stole in

the streets during the day, and found an abandoned building or a park bench to rest his head at night. At first, survival was Dre's main concern on the streets. On nights where he found himself with no food or money, he hung around restaurants, mostly Chinese and pizzerias during closing times, where he offered to help clean up in exchange for leftovers.

One day, while in the streets, Dre was starving and in a desperate search for a victim. He wandered into a park he frequented, where he spotted a young hustler clocking his numbers. Dre took a moment to blend in with the park visitors, observing the hustler for some time before making his move. Out of desperation, he closed the distance between himself and the hustler, still observing his moves.

Satisfied with his findings, he made a beeline towards the young hustler and demanded money. The hustler brushed him off, which was the worst thing he could've done. Without uttering another word, Dre rained blows on the hustler, knocking him to the ground. He proceeded to loot the young hustler's pockets for his pack and cash, and as he hurriedly made his exit from the park, laughed loudly while the young hustler cried, "Aah, my nose, my nose!"

Two weeks later, Dre was abducted as he roamed about the streets and taken inside a bodega. In the back of the corner store stood the young hustler and two older men. After the young hustler fingered Dre as the culprit, one of the older men interrogated him. Despite being out-numbered, he never panicked. In fact, he looked the older man dead in his eyes and told him the reason why he had done it.

For his bravery and honesty, the older man took a liking to Dre, offering him a job as a lookout, to which he accepted. Like a sponge to water, Dre absorbed knowledge from the older hustler. As a lookout, Dre continued to observe his surroundings and absorb knowledge from the older hustlers. In no time, Dre's boss was so impressed with his actions that he decided to give him a chance as a pitcher. Dre quickly excelled as a pitcher, moving up the ladder. It wasn't long before Dre developed into a smart young hustler, capable of handling his own packs.

Chapter 5: RISE AND GRIND

By age sixteen, Dre became an established young hustler and one of his boss' top earners. He also became well known by all the big timers in the neighborhood. A few of them even offered him better positions, more money and better incentives in an attempt to lure him to their respective cliques but Dre remained loyal to his boss. Because of Dre's unshaken loyalty, his boss continued to bless him, rewarding him with a studio apartment and his first hoopty — a Honda Accord.

More settled now, Dre made it his duty to get in touch with his brother Nine. Letters, commissary checks, and packages were just the beginning. He even managed to succeed in convincing a few girls to visit his brother in prison. Dre went on to retain a reputable attorney to handle his big brother's appeal.

One morning, Dre's boss invited him to his house for breakfast, which he gladly accepted. Instead of eggs and pancakes, however, his boss drove him to an unfamiliar block, where they made a pick up. The boss introduced him to several people while they were there. As they drove back, his boss said to him, "This here would soon be yours if you keep up the good work."

Dre, being no fool, seized the opportunity by working even harder to earn his prize. Within eight months, Dre set up shop on the new block with his own crew of young, levelheaded, and hungry hustlers. Dre personally selected Cash, the young hustler whom he had beat up and robbed in the park to be his second in command, a way to show his appreciation. With his own block and crew now, Dre's cash flow grew amazingly superb. He was finally living the life that he'd once dreamed of, comfortably and peacefully. Getting money became a full time job for Dre. Actually, getting money became his life.

It wasn't long before Dre caught the attention of a redbone named Tanya, who lived down the street from his new block. Two years Dre's senior, Tanya was a pretty little thing with a gorgeous face, flawless skin-tone, firm body, and long black hair that extended just below her shoulders. At about five-foot-tall and one-hundred-and-twenty-seven pounds, Tanya was simply a beauty with her long shapely legs, ample breasts, bubble butt, and a pair of hips to die for.

Dre flirted with Tanya on many occasions, just as he'd done with most of the girls that walked up and down his block. It wasn't long before Tanya lured him into her sweet garden. The two fell hard for each other and before long, shared Dre's studio apartment. A few months after Dre's eighteenth birthday, the two married, flying to Costa Rica for their honeymoon.

Despite being a married man, Dre's heart remained in the streets. They were all he knew and so he continued to live the street life, loving every bit of it. With money pouring in from his new block, he was able to move Tanya into a condominium and purchase a bigger apartment for his in-laws in a quiet neighborhood. Dre also acquired nearly half a dozen expensive cars without having as much as a learner's permit. With a little help from his boss and Tanya, Dre invested some of his earnings, opening two clothing stores as a start. Dre's status in the hood skyrocketed. The young kids admired him while the old timers respected him.

Over time, Dre became too obsessed with his riches. Starting off, he rented a few plush apartments around the city to accommodate his extra-marital activities. Dre purchased lots of expensive clothing and jewelry, as well as wining and dining different broads at fancy restaurants, night in and night out. He changed cars daily and absolutely refused to go out in public in the same outfit twice.

To Dre, the green piece of paper better known as a *dollar* was everything. Growing ridiculously obnoxious, Dre let his money speak for him every chance he got. Hell, rumors floated that during a night out drinking with his crew, he compared himself to John Gotti, the famous mob boss regarded for his expensive suits and flashy lifestyle.

Dre's new ways only garnered lots of negative attention from haters and the police alike, making him a target.

Chapter 6: THE PROPOSITION

"The coupe colored aquamarine, I got haze blocks..." The sound of Styles P's *Tryna Get Rich* seeped through the hoopty's speakers at a low volume. On this warm Saturday night, KD and Dolla found themselves in the crowded parking lot of Paradise, a recently opened strip club in the Hunts Point section of the Bronx. The assortment of vehicles in the parking lot was a sure indication that the place was packed, just as it had been since opening its doors three months ago.

"Yo, what's taking home-girl so long?" KD inquired as he took the spliff from Dolla.

"Chill, son, you know you can't rush perfection." Dolla shot back.

"Shit, all this waiting is making me nervous." KD said, sucking his teeth.

"Must be the haze. Here, pass that shit." Dolla teased, reaching for the spliff.

"Fuck outta here, homie! You better recognize who you're talking to." KD countered, taking another long pull on the spliff before passing it to Dolla.

To some of the perverted patrons of the gentlemen's club, it was just another night of throwing dollar bills at strippers. KD and Dolla, on the other hand, had a completely different agenda — one important enough to bring them out here on a Saturday night.

Cash, a hustler they knew from their neighborhood, invited them out tonight to "discuss a proposition." While they saw and interacted with Cash regularly, they didn't have an iota of trust for him. To them, he was an outsider, just like those who weren't part of their family. So sending Bebe, one of Dolla's girlfriends inside the club to play the mad wife looking for her husband was a good way to scope out the premises.

Having done enough cutthroat shit in their young lives, they couldn't be too cautious. They came prepared for the unexpected; they were both strapped with nine-millimeter pistols. In addition, wrapped in a blanket on the back seat of the hoopty was a short-barreled AK-47, equipped with extra magazines. If these young wolves hadn't learned anything in the streets, they've learned plenty about the disadvantages of being caught unprepared.

Nearly a half an hour went by and KD was getting anxious and impatient. Dolla's phone rang and he reached for it almost instantly. "Tell me something good, baby." He said into the phone.

KD, in the passenger seat, hung on to Dolla's every word, his anxiety level rising by the second. After an exchange with the caller, Dolla hung up, turned to KD, and asked, "You ready, son?"

KD let out a long sigh; obviously relieved things were still going according to plan.

The two continued to pass the spliff back and forth, as they watched Bebe stroll sexily across the parking lot to her Honda, the knocking of her stilettos in sync with the swaying of her sexy hips. Just as previously instructed, Bebe got in her car and peeled off with an attitude. It was as if someone was after her.

The two took another ten minutes to wrap up their smoking session before exiting the hoopty. Side by side, they took the short walk to the club's entrance. Paying their way inside had been a smooth process. Once inside, they proceeded directly to the bar area, checking for anything out of the ordinary. They saw nothing significantly odd so they seated themselves at the bar and ordered drinks — two double shot Hennessy. While KD waited and paid for their drinks, Dolla continued to look around.

"Look at this chump in the corner." Dolla said over the loud music as KD passed him his drink.

KD took a sip of his drink, following Dolla's gaze

towards the left hand corner of the club. Sure enough, he found himself looking at Cash, pre-occupied with two dancers in a corner booth. Slowly, they sipped their drinks and kept an indirect eye on Cash, occasionally checking the rest of the club for anything suspicious. To avoid looking obvious, they occupied themselves with two dancers, who were very happy to have made their company.

When Cash finally saw them from his booth, he left the dancers and headed over to the bar area. He approached and excused himself before giving the two daps and asking, "Y'all been here long?"

"Nah, we just walked in." Dolla answered quickly.

"I got a booth for us over there," said Cash as he signaled towards his corner booth, where the two dancers awaited.

KD and Dolla agreed to join Cash before he walked off, pausing at the bar to whisper something to the blond bartender. Paying and dismissing their dancers moments later, KD and Dolla downed the rest of their drinks and headed in the direction of Cash's booth. Upon their arrival, Cash tipped his two dancers and told them they had five more minutes to hang out with him. It was obvious that Cash had built a rapport with the employees of Paradise from the way he interacted with them. For the few minutes, the three men enjoyed their lap dances. When the dancers realized that their presence was no longer required, they thanked Cash and went on their way.

"Gentlemen, I'm glad y'all could make it," said Cash over the loud music.

"Yea, I hope this doesn't take long." KD shot back in response, paying close attention to Cash's movements.

Dolla continued to scan the place, using the thick Spanish dancer on stage as a decoy. Moments later, a burly dark-skinned man in a black t-shirt with the word, "STAFF" printed in white across the back approached, and asked the three to follow him. Dolla gave KD the *stay on point* look, and KD returned with the same. They gained an advantage from growing up with one another — communication using only their facial expressions. The burly man ushered the three down a hallway and upstairs to one of their private rooms.

Now seated on plush couches in the privacy of the room, their glasses filled courtesy of the bottle service included in the cost of the room, Cash officially broke the ice by shaking their hands one more time and saying, "Once again, gentlemen, I'm glad y'all could make it."

KD and Dolla both acknowledged with a head nod.

"As you know," Cash continued, "I called you here tonight to discuss a proposition."

KD and Dolla looked at each other, then back to Cash with curious faces. Knowing the hustler that Cash was, they were ready to hear more about his proposition, as they knew money would be involved. They just couldn't pinpoint what Cash would require in return, and that was the reason they had taken time out of their Saturday night to meet with him.

Cash, noticing their reaction, continued to speak, "I believe I found a way for all of us to eat together."

"We're all ears, Cash Money," said Dolla impatiently.

"Dre!" Cash simply said.

"What about Dre?" KD spoke up quickly, obviously unsatisfied with the riddling manner in which Cash was carrying on the meeting.

"I know how much y'all can't stand his guts," Cash paused and took a sip of his drink before adding, "Well, we all have something in common."

KD and Dolla looked at each other in confusion, then back at Cash as they tried to decipher which direction he was headed with the conversation.

"Y'all know I run Grant but Dre is my boss," Cash clasped his hands together and leaned forward as he spoke. "I'm on the block all day, making sure shit runs right and that flashy muthafucka ain't giving me what I deserve," he finally blurted out.

"Are you saying what I think you're saying?" KD snapped with a puzzled look on his face.

"All I'm saying is this, homie: if we get rid of Dre,

the block and the workers are up for the taking!" Said Cash with conviction as he looked from KD to Dolla and back to KD.

KD and Dolla looked at each other and nodded slowly in agreement with Cash. There were some questions, however, that needed to be answered. For all they knew, Dre could be using Cash to test them. Dolla spoke first after taking a drink of yak from his glass. "I see your point, but why bring us in?" Asked Dolla.

"Aye, I'm just a hustler, homie. I ain't about that dirty work." Cash responded.

KD took a sip of his drink and shot a suspicious look. He didn't like the direction in which the conversation was headed. *What does he mean by dirty work?* Wondered KD before asking, "Ok, but why us, though?"

"I know how y'all get down, homie. Besides, I know y'all probably dislike him even more now for that shit that happened a while back." Cash shot back quickly.

While the situation started to make sense to KD and Dolla, it came across as tricky all the same. Some months back, KD, Dolla, and Poundz started moving haze for Dre, to make a little pocket money and support their smoking habits. Somehow, Black, KD's uncle, found out about it and gave Dre more than an earful. Since Black became Dre's new connect after his boss' death, Dre had no choice but to swallow his pride and cut the young boys loose. This incident tarnished their relationship with Dre forever.

"Let's say we agree to go through with this, what exactly is in it for us?" Dolla asked, leaning forward as if to emphasize his question.

"Well, we can agree to a 50/50 partnership or we can make other arrangements when the time comes," responded Cash without hesitation.

A smirk appeared on Dolla's face, which told KD exactly what he needed to know — a 50/50 split sounded good but Cash would have to settle for whatever they gave him or he'd join his boss.

"Your proposition sounds good, Cash Money," KD continued to pry for answers, "But how do we know you're not lining us up?"

If they were to make this happen, then they needed to rule out any and all possibilities.

"K, all I'm saying is that I deserve much better for the amount of work I put in and Dre don't seem to understand that." Cash answered.

Something about the way Cash answered the question made KD believe him. Yet, he didn't trust him. To give Cash the benefit of the doubt, KD offered his best, "Cash Money, we gonna need to think about this. I mean this is a major move."

Before KD could finish his statement, Dolla and Cash both nodded in agreement. Although, it was obvious that Cash wasn't hoping for this response, it was better than a no. It was important that they all understood the magnitude of the situation. There'd be a lot of work involved should they agree to move forward. For this move to be successful, they would have to leave no stones unturned.

After giving it some thought, Cash agreed with the arrangement by shaking hands with KD and Dolla.

"We'll be in touch," said KD as he raised his glass.

Dolla and Cash followed suit. The three men gripped their glasses and downed the contents.

"Y'all gonna stay and have some fun or what?" Cash asked with excitement.

"One more drink," responded Dolla.

"And maybe a dance," added KD, laughing aloud.

Dolla refilled their glasses while Cash used the room's intercom system to request some dancers. For the next half an hour, the men enjoyed drinks and lap dances from three beautiful and curvaceous dancers. When they were satisfied, KD and Dolla left Cash to enjoy the rest of his night.

From Paradise, they drove back to Grant Avenue, where they stashed their guns. They then called Bebe to come get them for the house party she was having at her apartment. While they waited for Bebe's arrival at their usual spot in front of their building, they each rolled up a spliff and sipped on a half-empty bottle of Hennessy they bought earlier that day.

Bebe came from around the corner after about fifteen minutes, honking her horn as if she didn't see the two sitting at their usual spot. The two joined Bebe in her Accord, Dolla in the front seat with KD occupying the back. Before Bebe could pull off, Dolla said, "I hope your party is jumping, Be."

"Word, I hope you got some beauties over there for me," KD chimed in.

Bebe simply gave KD a look of disgust as she peeled off.

Chapter 7: THE PUZZLE

In the days following the meeting with Cash, KD, Dolla, and Poundz collectively conducted a series of extensive footwork, not only on Dre, but on Cash as well. The idea that Dre could be using Cash to get to them surfaced in nearly every conversation the three had. Then there was this personal vendetta, which they discovered in the process that Cash had against Dre. Word on the streets was that an incident took place in a park some years back, where Cash received a beat down from Dre.

Considering this factor, the last thing they wanted was for Cash to trick them into taking out Dre for his own personal benefit. That'd be the ultimate disrespect. They hadn't lived in the hood all these years just to play someone else's puppets, especially after going to such great length to plant their feet. Even at their relatively young age, their track record in the hood was remarkable. The last thing they wanted was to have their reputation damaged.

The only certainty they saw in this situation was that Cash wasn't about gunplay. Thus, when it was all said and done, if need be they would handle him as well. A natural-born hustler, Cash could sell garlic to a vampire; hence his moniker. That one quality made Cash valuable. Yet, the hood was a place where you never knew what was cooking in the next man's pot. You could laugh with a man today and he'll be the same one robbing you tomorrow.

"Any man, whether weak or strong, smart or dumb, if pushed hard enough, is bound to react." The list of possibilities ran endless, which compelled them to resort to the process of elimination. In the initial stages, they concluded that opening up to Cash a bit more would be helpful. They needed to get a feel for him and there was no better way of going about it than to get closer to him.

Gradually, they befriended Cash, going clubbing together on numerous occasions. They would invite Cash to join them in their smoking sessions and even make sports bets against one another. In so doing, not only did they establish some level of trust but it also gave them a better idea of Cash's position in the situation. Within a few short weeks, they had an idea from which angle to approach the situation.

Then there was Dre, who was a very different animal. With Dre, there was no hanging out, which made it nearly impossible to get close to him. First, there was the age difference, then there was the fact that he thought so

THE GENESIS

highly of himself. Yet, they found a solution to their problem by the name of Suzie. Suzie was an ex- girlfriend of KD's from way back.

KD and Suzie dated for some years until she decided to move to Atlanta after high school. They ended their relationship on a good note but when Suzie returned to New York after things hadn't worked out down south, KD had moved on. The two maintained a cordial relationship since. A college student by day and a stripper by night, Suzie was the precious gem they lacked, the missing piece to their puzzle. "I'm just doing it long enough to put myself through college." Suzie would always say when asked about her profession. Nonetheless, calling on Suzie for a favor wasn't a bad idea.

A little bit of digging revealed that Suzie became one of Dre's favorite dancers. Their work had really paid off when KD discovered that Dre and Suzie had an ongoing, no strings arrangement. Initially, Suzie was reluctant about giving KD information but with a little persuasion, she gave in. Suzie knew Dre was a married man but she also knew that he was a baller and as long as he paid for her condo and splurged on her, she was fine with their affair. To her, Dre was just another meal ticket.

Chapter 8: GROUNDWORK

Days turned into weeks, and weeks into months while the trio tried to navigate their way through life. Having made the decision earlier on that the street life was their future, finding a substantial hustle was their main focus. To them, it was one thing to grow up in the hood but their plan was to rise above that by any means necessary. With their level of discipline, they could accomplish this task with grave effort. It was their attitude to do things their way that proved to be a setback.

Hell, they heard plenty of stories about people just like themselves, rising up out of the slums to pursue and achieve their dreams. They knew of athletes and celebrities who had risen above the hood and achieved success in their careers.

Yet, they viewed themselves as lacking role models and the proper backing. In all honesty, they idolized the gangstas and the hustlers that they encountered. Fancy cars, the women and jewelry, the flashy lifestyle in general enticed them. They viewed these individuals as role models and aspired to be like them, if not better.

KD knew his uncle Black, whom he viewed as a role model, was a businessman, but he also knew that not all his businesses were legal. He had plans to pursue the same path that Black had, but since Black made it clear to him earlier on that he didn't support that decision, he saw fit to create his own path. With Dolla and Poundz at his side, he felt he could take over the world. They understood that success came with hard work, and they were prepared to go the extra mile.

This was one of the reasons that they took interest in Cash's proposition. If done right, they knew their future could be brighter. It was just a matter of how to go about it. While they could approach Dre with the get-down-or-lay-down mentality, they also understood that it wouldn't be the most effective approach. Their only other choice was to get rid of Dre. While this was a risky approach, it was also the most beneficial. At this point, they had more than what they needed to make it happen; it was a matter of solidifying things.

They had another sit-down with Cash, this time bringing Poundz into the fold. They ironed out their proposition and came to an agreement during this second meeting. If things went as planned, Cash would assume Dre's position as boss and owner of the operation. The trio would remain silent partners with Cash, each of whom would have a twenty-five percent stake. As far as a supplier, KD had his sights set on Black. With or without Dre, Black wouldn't be too keen to lose his income from the operation, he concluded. They deduced a plan B in the event that Black decided to walk away.

Chapter 9: HIT' EM UP

"Yo, this is some good ass piff, son," Dolla called from the rear seat.

"Word, this is some fire! Who you got this from, K?" Poundz chimed in.

KD remained silent, his eyes glued to the fourth floor window of the building. Though he was partaking in the *puff puff pass* ritual, his main focus was on getting the job at hand done, and done right.

The smoke-filled van they occupied that night was dark blue in color. Strategically parked among the assortment of vehicles that lined both sides of the street, the van looked perfectly in place. With its ignition off, the only source of light and sound were the orange tip of the spliff in rotation and the pot-headed chitchat between Dolla and Poundz. From the front passenger seat, KD monitored their target, while Poundz and Dolla occupied the driver and rear seats respectively.

Prior to being brought on this trip, the van, stolen days earlier, had undergone a makeover — new license plates, designs on the rear fenders, darker tints on the windows and bumper stickers, two of which read *Soccer Mom* and *Proud Parent of a College Graduate*. A little humor could be appreciated no matter the situation, or so they thought.

The day was a Saturday but they didn't care what time or day of the week it was. All they knew was that they had the drop on Dre and were going to ride on him. Having waited a long time for their opportunity, they refused to let it slip by them. Since their meeting with Cash at Paradise, they had been hard at work, and now, more than six months later, they could say that they had Dre's movements down pat.

The pot-headed chitchat continued between Dolla and Poundz. "Yo, you good, K?" Dolla inquired.

Silence.

"Word, you awfully quiet over there. Let me find out you got the butterflies or some shit," teased Poundz with his slick self.

"Just make sure y'all ready to go when the time comes," KD finally snapped. Similar to the quiet before the storm, he was in a zone of his own, waiting for the right moment to strike.

"My joint always on point," Dolla shot back, caressing the silenced 9 millimeter pistol that laid on the seat next to him.

The trio continued to pass the spliff among themselves while they awaited for their cue. KD checked the time on his watch, 12:35 a.m. *Suzie needs to hurry up.* He thought to himself.

Deep in his thoughts, KD was amazed at how he'd been able to manipulate Suzie into becoming part of the situation. At the outset, he'd played the concerned friend role, constantly hinting that Suzie deserved better than being a sidepiece. This led Suzie to ask for the number one spot, although she knew Dre was a married man. She developed a sudden hatred for Dre when she discovered she was just another piece of pussy to him, hence her easy recruitment. The cherry on top was that KD convinced her to move back to Atlanta after tonight. With a new identity and the decent amount of cash that he'd promised her, she'd be able to reestablish herself and continue her hustle in some of the big strip clubs there.

Still in thought, KD was getting ready to talk shit to Dolla when, through the passenger side-view mirror of the van, he spotted an NYPD patrol car creeping up. Almost instantaneously, he was back on high alert. For starters, if the stolen van wasn't enough, they had enough illegal guns and ammunition to land the three of them in the slammer for a lifetime. *We'd just have to take our chances and hold court in the streets.* Thought KD.

"Yo, get low!" KD warned.

As if on cue, all three men depressed in their respective seats, as the patrol car crept past, continued down the block, and turned right at the corner.

"Good eyes, K," Poundz commended once the patrol car was out of sight.

"Word!" Dolla added.

"Keep your eyes open just in case they circle around," KD warned his partners. There was no need to get complacent after doing all the groundwork.

At 2:20 a.m., KD's cell buzzed with a text message. He opened the message to reveal a smiley face, the cue they had been waiting for. A smile appeared on his own face.

"Game time," was all he said before taking one last look at the fourth floor window. Just as planned, KD exited the van with Dolla, leaving Poundz in the driver's seat as a lookout. Doing their best not to look suspicious, the two proceeded side by side to their target building. To help conceal their guns, KD wore a grey Champion hoodie and a black Sean Jean leather coat, while Dolla donned a black three-quarter length leather trench coat. With the spare set of keys Suzie gave KD, they had no problem gaining access into the building.

Once inside the building, they took the elevator to the third floor, looking every bit as if they belonged there. They exited the elevator and quickly proceeded to the third floor stairway, where they staged in final preparation for their attack in the fourth floor apartment. Step after step, they climbed two flights to the fourth floor landing, where they paused shortly to survey for signs of activity. Satisfied with their findings, they donned their black skullies and leather gloves.

Just like they had done on many occasions, they inspected each other and assured their readiness with a fist bump. It was game time! KD led the way into the hallway, a silenced pistol drawn. Dolla brought in the rear, two pistols at the ready. Quietly, they crept towards apartment four D, which was the last door to the left. KD positioned himself on the right side of the door while Dolla took the position across from him. With a gloved hand, KD tried the doorknob and it turned freely. No need for a key after all.

He looked at Dolla for a signal, to which Dolla responded with a nod. KD turned the knob again, this time slowly pushing the door inward just wide enough for them to enter. With the quickness of a well-trained military man, Dolla led the way with his two pistols, ready to eliminate any immediate threats. KD followed suit, quietly shutting the door behind them. The darkness in the apartment caused a moment of blindness but their eyes quickly readjusted.

They could hear the sound of video games from their right, where a ray of light illuminated a hallway. KD drew his second silenced pistol and followed Dolla down the short hallway, which led to the living room. There, a familiar man sat on a couch, playing video games. Loco, Dre's longtime bodyguard had been caught unprepared. At the sight of them, Loco dropped his controller and quickly reached for his weapon. He wasn't quick enough, however, because Dolla was in his face with two pistols, ready to splatter his brains.

They heard the voice of Trey Songs from a room to the right. With quickness, KD moved on Loco. Removing his gun from his reach, KD quickly and quietly bound Loco's hands behind him with a roll of duct tape from his coat pocket. He then sat Loco down on the couch, bound his ankles and sealed his lips with a piece of tape. Satisfied, KD signaled for Dolla to keep an eye on Loco while he searched the rest of the apartment.

With his two silenced pistols, KD followed the sound of Trey Songs to the room's door. He checked the doorknob, which turned with ease. Pushing the door open, he entered the room ready for action. There, awaited their prize — Dre sleeping like a baby with Suzie lying next to him.

THE GENESIS

"Wake up, muthafucka!" Barked KD as he nudged Dre upside the head with the barrel of one of his pistols.

Still half-asleep, Dre turned and mumbled something that ended with, "baby."

"Get the fuck up, chump!" KD bellowed, smacking Dre in the back of the head with the butt of one of his pistols.

Dre got the picture then because he was wide awake, holding his head and staring at two silenced pistols. Dre, obviously confused, looked from KD to Suzie, who scurried into one corner of the bed. The expression on her face was one of absolute fright.

"Please, don't hurt me, please..." A half-naked Suzie pleaded but KD silenced her with a swing of one of his pistols in her direction.

"Fuck you want, homie?" Still a bit confused, Dre asked nonchalantly.

"Fuck up, pussy! I'm doing the talking here," responded KD before adding, "Do as I say and nobody will get hurt." He then removed the roll of duct tape from his pocket. "Here, tape his hands up," instructed KD, tossing the tape to Suzie.

Dre looked from KD to Suzie, then back to KD.

"Bitch, hurry up!" Barked KD, obviously unimpressed with the speed of Suzie.

"You gotta be shitting me," Dre said, shaking his head.

"One more word from you and I'mma make you hurt," KD said firmly before looking at Suzie and adding, "You, hurry up!"

Slowly, Suzie moved towards Dre and began to apply the tape to his wrists.

"To the back!" Barked KD, his pistols still trained on the two lovers.

Reluctantly, Dre allowed Suzie to bind his wrists tightly behind his back.

"To the living room, both of you, c'mon. Let's go!" KD barked, signaling for them to leave the bedroom with his pistols.

Frightened as all hell, Suzie followed Dre out of the bedroom, her tears flowing freely down her dimpled cheeks. KD marched the two into living room, where Dolla and Loco awaited.

"You, sit down!" KD barked at Dre before turning to Suzie and adding, "And you, get over there!"

Suzie did as instructed before balling up in one corner of the couch next to Dre and Loco.

"C'mon, all this shit ain't necessary, man. If it's money y'all want, I'll give it to you. Just don't hurt us," pleaded Dre as he sat defenseless in his boxers.

Just then, KD peeled his skully back, exposing his face.

"Yo, I know this ain't..." Dre started but a hard blow to the face from KD silenced him.

"Let's try this again, shut the fuck up!" KD barked but Dre was too busy in pain to even acknowledge him.

"Matter of fact, let me see the tape." Dolla said with anger as he placed a piece of tape over Dre's mouth.

Witnessing this, Suzie bawled her eyes out. It was as if her life was in real danger. *Damn, she deserves an Oscar for that act.* Thought KD.

"Listen up, Dre," KD started before adding, "A little birdie told me your bitch ass is getting a lot of money and since I ain't seeing none of it, this is what we're gonna do."

"Mmm mmm mmm," Dre managed to stifle through the duct tape.

"Whatchu got to say?" KD taunted.

"Mmm mmm, mmm mmm," Stifled Dre as he nodded his head up and down.

"Whatchu got to say?" KD asked, peeling the duct tape off Dre's mouth.

"If is money y'all came for then we can work something out, just don't hurt us, K." Dre managed in one long sentence.

"Yo, you heard this fool?" KD asked Dolla, chuckling as if Dre just told the funniest joke.

"At least let her go, she ain't got nothing to do with this," pleaded Dre.

"Whatchu got to trade for her?" Dolla demanded.

"Take me to my stash house and y'all can have whatever y'all want," Dre responded.

At the sound of that, Dolla yanked Suzie onto the floor and pointed one of his pistols at her head to show Dre he meant business. Dre turned his head away but KD wasn't having that. KD grabbed and turned Dre's head to a distressed Suzie.

"Don't fuck with me if you love your bitch!" KD barked holding Dre's head firmly in the direction of Suzie.

Dre became teary eyed as he watched Suzie cry her heart out, her head mere inches away from the barrel of Dolla's pistol.

"Ok, ok! I got two bricks and some cash in the kitchen. Take the gun off her and y'all can have that," pleaded Dre through tears.

"Getcha bitch ass up and show me where it is!" KD barked, hoisting Dre up by his left arm.

With one pistol tucked and the other jammed deep into Dre's ribcage, KD allowed Dre to lead him to a small freezer in the kitchen. Upon arrival, KD attempted to open the freezer just to find out it was a dummy. The fucking thing was a safe!

"What do we have here?" KD taunted before adding, "Nice one! How do you open this bitch?"

Dre pretended not to hear KD. In response, KD jammed the pistol deeper into his ribcage, making him grimace.

"Do you love that bitch in there?" KD asked Dre.

"You got it, you got it!" Dre finally said before showing KD a secret keypad.

"What's the code, Dre?" KD asked, pushing on the pistol.

"Try 00826060#."

KD tried it but got nowhere. That earned Dre another blow to the head. Dre screamed out in pain before spitting out the right code. KD tried it and bam, the door popped open. Inside the small safe were three kilos of pure cocaine, two kilos of heroin and some cash. KD quickly pulled out a sack from his back pocket and emptied the contents into it while Dre watched on with the look of death in his eyes.

"What else you got around here?" KD asked Dre.

"That's everything, man, y'all gon' let us go now?" Dre countered with a question of his own.

"Shut ya bitch ass up!" KD barked, dragging Dre to the living room and shoving him back on the couch. He replaced the piece of tape over Dre's mouth before adding with conviction, "If I find anything else in this house, you, your man, and that bitch will be history."

KD then stormed off to the bedroom. In there, he searched thoroughly. From dresser drawers to closets to suitcases. He even flipped the mattress on the bed but his search revealed nothing much. He proceeded to the kitchen where he searched the cabinets and drawers, still nothing. He returned to the living room where he made the three victims sit on the floor while he flipped and searched the couches. Still nothing.

Satisfied, it was time for them to make their exit. As planned, they would be taking Suzie with them as a prisoner. But first, they had to do one last thing.

"You, get dressed!" KD barked to Suzie, who literally ran to the bedroom to retrieve her belongings.

She barely made it to the bedroom when KD nodded to Dolla. As if on cue, they both grabbed a cushion from the couch. Placing the cushions over Dre and Loco, KD and Dolla squeezed two shots each into their chests, killing them at once. Suzie reemerged from the bedroom shortly thereafter, and after collecting the sack of drugs and cash, the three left the apartment. With their guns concealed under their outer garments, they walked out of the building casually, joined Poundz in the van outside, and drove off into the darkness. Dolla placed a call to the Ramirez twins from high school — the clean-up crew. They were more than happy to get rid of the bodies and any mess left behind in Dre's apartment.

Chapter 10: BLACK

Nearly two weeks went by since the hit on Dre and things were quiet for the most part. KD, Dolla, and Poundz remained low-key, keeping their movements normal and to a minimum. Suzie left for Atlanta the same night after receiving thirty- five of the one-hundred-and-five-thousand dollars taken from Dre's safe. The Ramirez brothers cleaned up every nook and cranny of Dre's apartment, and for their work, they received a healthy payment.

More talks with Cash had taken place immediately following the hit. So far, everyone involved in the situation was well aware of the arrangements. Cash would step up to fill Dre's shoes, while appointing himself a next in command to fill his own. Concerning their role in the operation, KD, Dolla, and Poundz would serve as silent partners and call shots from behind the scenes. Having agreed on an equal stake of twenty-five percent each with Cash retaining the remaining twenty-five percent, things were moving according to plan.

With the drugs taken from Dre's safe, and what Cash had left at the stash house, they looked to be in good position for the next few months. Their next move was to find a solid connect, who would supply them consistently. That's what made Black KD's ace in the whole. Being that Black was Dre's connect, KD planned to use his family ties to cash in on the opportunity. Should his plan backfire, they had a plan B and even a plan C. Dolla and Poundz knew that their cousin Gordo's father was the man when it came to the coke game, and they planned to use that to their advantage.

Lounging about, burning spliff after spliff with his brothers, KD ran lines through his head. Lines about how he'd deliver the news to Black. They were fortunate enough for Black to agree on a meeting with them that evening, and they intended to make the most of it. The meeting, which was to take place at Black's nightclub at midnight, was drawing nearer. Together, the three young men prepared themselves to meet with Black.

At about a quarter of eleven, the three set off on the short drive to the nightspot. KD's hoopty — a golden-brown 1996 Cadillac Seville — served as their means of transportation for the night. The three rode in silence the entire way, which was unlike them. It was evident that the magnitude of the meeting and the message they carried weighed on them. Arriving at about a quarter past eleven, they entered the place through the rear entrance.

As always, Black was happy to see them, as evident by the strong hugs he showered them. Present with Black was his longtime friend and shooter, Danja. A tough as nails son-of-a-bitch, Danja and Black had a history which dated back to the beginning of Black's criminal career. Danja was his usual jovial self, cracking jokes on the three young men the moment they walked in and saluted him. To best set the mood, the yak flowed generously and the spliffs stayed lit.

The five men sat at a roundtable, chitchatting about life as they engaged in a friendly poker game in the backroom of the club. That only lasted until Black suddenly asked, "What's so important that you wanted to talk to me about?"

With that, the meeting was formally underway. The jokes and chitchats suddenly ceased. KD looked from Dolla to Poundz, then Danja to Black. He then cleared his throat before speaking.

"Unk, we have a situation on our hands that we need your help with," KD said, gesturing towards Dolla and Poundz who sat on opposite sides of him.

Black, with a raised brow looked the three young men in the face, from one to the other before speaking.

"And what exactly are we talking about?" He asked.

"Well, Unk," KD started before adding, "I know we've been down this road before but this time, things are a little different."

Black knew just where his nephew was headed with the conversation so he cut right to the chase.

"Just what makes it different this time?" He asked.

"Unk, Dre's block is officially ours," blurted KD.

Black looked at his nephew puzzled. He looked to Danja for answers but Danja appeared even more confused.

"Let's just say Dre is no longer with us, Unk," KD used the opportunity to explain.

The look that appeared on Black's face after hearing his nephew was possibly the most serious that the three young men had ever seen.

"Just what on earth is that supposed to mean?" Asked Black, his tone rising a decibel.

KD looked dead in his uncle's eyes and spoke, this time in a much calmer but firm tone, "Dre had something that we needed, Unk, so we took it."

Black leaned back in his seat, his eyes wide open as he gazed unbelievably at the three young men. Danja, on the other hand, crossed his hands and leaned forward, resting his elbows on the table. The shocking news coupled with KD's attitude caught the older men by utter surprise. For a moment, no one said a word. No sound was made, just blank looks on all five faces. The tension in the room was thicker than a forty-pound piece of beef. Clearly not the reaction the young men expected.

Black was the first to break the awkward silence. "Just so I understand you correctly," he began before asking, "What exactly have you done?"

"As I said earlier, Unk, Dre is no longer with us." KD cleared his throat before speaking, his nervousness as clear as daylight. He wasn't one to get nervous, but facing blank stares from legends like Black and Danja got the best of him.

Danja shook his head but did not say a word. Dolla and Poundz, like Danja, had yet to speak since the meeting officially began. This was exactly how they planned to carry out the meeting.

"When did this happen?" Black asked firmly. "Two weeks ago." KD replied.

"And the body?" Black asked.

"It's been taken care of," KD replied then added firmly, "We've cleaned up well. No evidence was left behind and definitely no traces."

Black let out a long sigh, rubbing his face with his palms. It was clearly not a sigh of relief, more like one of disappointment. He thought for a moment before speaking, "What have you come to me for? What exactly do you need from me?" He asked crossing his hands over his chest. It was obvious that the news wasn't sitting well with him.

"I need the same relationship you and Dre had, Unk, or maybe even better," responded KD with confidence. He and his brothers were determined to win, and whether Black was impressed with their actions or not, they needed him to be a connection, not an uncle.

Black looked at Danja and let out another long sigh. He understood that he'd lost the battle of sheltering his nephew from the street life. It was obvious that KD was carving his own path through life. Black now faced the task of supporting and guiding his nephew through the treacherous terrain better known as the streets.

"I hope you understand what you're getting yourself into, nephew. This life is not one of glamor but rather, one of treachery. Loyalty and discipline could take you a long way, but having the right eyes and ears around you is just as important. I can't make no promises but I'll sleep on it," Black finally ended his speech.

Danja and the three young men nodded in agreement.

"Thanks, Unk, this means a lot to us," KD said, pointing to Dolla and Poundz.

"In the meantime, you keep your eyes and ears open," Black said before adding, "anything comes up, you let me know straightaway!"

"You got it, Unk! You'll not regret this, I promise," KD replied confidently.

"One last thing," Black said, rising from his seat. He then added, knocking on the table for emphasis, "You don't speak on what you shared with us to another soul, understood?" With that, he walked off in the direction of his office with Danja in tow. That was obviously the end of the meeting.

Chapter 11: THE CREW

Following their meeting with Black, the next thing on their agenda was to meet with Cash and iron out the new rules under which their operation would run. Having discussed the details amongst themselves, it was just a matter of presenting it to Cash, who would in turn relay it to his crew. The three understood that the best way to run a smooth operation was by making sure that crewmembers were on the same page, from Cash down to the foot soldiers.

About a month went by since they made their move on Dre. Rumors circulated about Dre's disappearance but nothing concrete. Nothing close enough to even indicate their involvement. Without a body, the whole thing remained a mystery, just as they had wished. The three continued to lay low for the most part. They couldn't afford any type of unnecessary heat. It was time to put their plan in full motion and take things to the next level as they had been planning for years.

Judging from Black's reaction and his response to them during the meeting, things weren't looking too bad. The worse that could happen at that point was that Black denied them, which seemed quite unlikely. Should that happen, they would just have to explore their other options. As far as product, they were still looking good to survive another month or two. With the money they took from Dre as well as that from the drugs, they had more than enough.

A Sunday night meeting took place at Paradise, the same location they had their first meeting. The only difference this time was that they made sure to arrive before Cash. While they had developed a relationship with Cash, they only trusted him to an extent. They still didn't want to take chances with him. At the end of the day, the hood was still the hood and partners or not, they knew the type of cat Cash was.

It was during that meeting that the young men solidified their partnership with Cash. They also agreed on an equal twenty-five percent stake for each one of them. With the amount of money that was coming in from the operation, twenty-five percent seemed more than a fair amount. Everyone was satisfied with the arrangement and transition. When Cash mentioned that they meet the crew, KD quickly declined. For the time being, they were silent partners and KD made sure to emphasize that point.

The four ended the meeting on a positive note, capping the night off in a celebratory fashion.

Chapter 12: KAREN

KD woke up to somebody's hands groping the lower part of his abdomen. Karen, his lovely girlfriend, just couldn't seem to get enough of him. Hell, he wouldn't have it any other way. In fact, any other way and he'd suspect her of being unfaithful. They were both stark naked underneath the soft woolen covers from the night before. Although he and Karen didn't see each other much since she'd gone off to college, when they did, they managed to make the most of it.

"Hey, baby," he greeted, leaning in for a kiss. The two shared a long passionate kiss, morning breath and all, Karen's left hand massaging in between his legs. He was hard as a rock. Karen straddled him and covered every inch of his face with kisses from her soft lips. She sucked on his neck and nibbled on his earlobes, whispering, "I love you, K," into his ears. Palming and massaging her thick juicy booty with both hands, KD did his best not to interrupt what his girl was doing.

Karen continued to plant kisses from his chest down to his abdomen, letting her tongue do tricks on his six-pack. Her soft round breasts brushed against his manhood and for a second, he thought he was going to explode. *Not yet, not so soon*, he thought to himself. Starting from the top of his thighs, she continued to kiss her way to his inner thighs. Finally, settling on his manhood, she gripped and stroked his thickness in her right hand.

She encircled the tip of his manhood with her tongue, causing him to let out a soft moan. Taking his manhood into her mouth, Karen pleased her man with the skill of a professional, sucking and stroking at the same time. KD was on top of the world and wished he could stay there forever. As much as he tried to prolong her performance, he couldn't hold his nut any longer. He came after about ten minutes and he came hard.

It was now his turn to reciprocate the favor. He flipped Karen onto her back, kissing and sucking on her neck. From there, he proceeded to her perky round breasts, admiring her natural feminine beauty. Karen was one beautiful young lady and KD was glad she was all his. He encircled his tongue around her hardened nipples and Karen urged him on with her sweet moans. Alternating from one to the other, he continued to give her breasts and nipples some special attention, licking, nibbling, sucking, and massaging them.

He moved lower, planting kisses all over Karen's flat stomach, all the while massaging her breasts with his hands. Oh how he loved the feel of her smooth flat stomach. When he reached below the belt, her legs opened to welcome him.

"Mmm," Karen panted when he slipped his middle finger into her kitty kat. She was soaking wet, which told him he had been doing his job. He moved his finger in and out, causing her to arch her back and grind her hips. Removing his finger from her kitty kat, he tasted his baby's love juices. Karen tasted sweet.

At that point, he knew he had to swoop in for the kill. He wanted Karen to have dreams of this episode, just as she'd had in the past. He started sucking and nibbling on her inner thighs, making her moan in pleasure. He knew this drove her wild so he spent some time there as her anticipation continued to build. Finally, he decided to switch positions. Lying on his back, he eased Karen onto his face as he attacked her love box.

First, he took his time to part her pussy lips, and then he stuck his tongue inside and gave it a suck. Karen cried out in ecstasy as her sweet juices flowed freely onto his tongue. In a circular motion, he twirled his tongue around her clit as he moved his middle finger in and out of her love box.

"I hate you, daddy! I fucking hate you!" Karen moaned in her sweetest little-girl voice but that only motivated KD. Grabbing the headboard for support, Karen grinded her hips onto KD's face.

Before long, Karen's legs started to shake and her body convulsed. KD knew he was winning the battle so he continued to lick her clit even faster, bringing her to an orgasm so intense that she repeatedly screamed out, "I love you, K! I fucking love you!"

When the smoke cleared, Karen had one hand full of KD's dreadlocks while she supported her weak legs with the other on the headboard. While Karen basked in the afterglow of their lovemaking, KD rolled a fat spliff of haze and headed straight for the bathroom. Lighting the spliff, he decided to run the shower. He sat atop the toilet seat, enjoying his spliff when Karen walked sexily inside the bathroom, looking like she was ready for round two. They shared the remainder of the spliff and got in the hot shower together.

Was it the effects of the spliff or the heat from the hot shower, or maybe a combination of both, but Karen's body looked even more delicious. He couldn't keep his hands off her flawless body. Their bodies quickly became one under the hot shower, their lips exploring the contours of each other's mouth. Before they realized, they were making love under the steaming hot water. Their lovemaking only lasted about fifteen minutes. They soaped and scrubbed each other's body afterwards.

Karen rinsed off first, leaving KD in the shower, where he stayed a little while longer. When he finally emerged from the bathroom, Karen yelled something to him about breakfast. He went inside the bedroom and put on some lotion, wrapped himself up in his white robe and joined Karen at the dining table, where they had breakfast together.

Over eggs, turkey bacon, wheat toast, and OJ, Karen decided to finally express her concern to her man. "K, I have something to talk to you about," she started.

"Talk to me, baby, what's wrong?" KD asked with concern. The last thing he wanted to hear was her being pregnant or something similar. While that wouldn't be bad news, it was definitely not the right time in their young lives, considering her education, among other things.

"Nothing is wrong, K. I just have some news that I think you'll find interesting," said Karen.

KD put down his fork and clasped his hands in front of him, giving his lady his undivided attention.

"You know I love you right, K?" Karen asked before adding, "I'm just concerned about you in the streets."

KD reached for Karen's left hand before speaking. "Baby-girl, I understand your concern but things are not as bad as you think. Trust me!" KD said encouragingly.

A small smile appeared on Karen's face upon hearing that. She took a sip of her orange juice then said, "I'm just concerned. I hate the thought of losing you to the streets."

"Baby listen, I'm not going anywhere so you don't have to worry about losing me," KD said with conviction. He knew that's not what she wanted to hear but that's all he could muster at that moment.

"I hear you, K," Karen started before adding, "But here is my suggestion. You don't have to act on it but at least hear me out."

KD had a slight idea of what was to follow. They had similar conversations in the past.

"Baby, you know I value your opinions," He said, preparing himself for the worse.

"Brownville, the small town where my college is," Karen started before adding, "There is an opportunity there for what you're into."

KD looked on puzzled. In response, he said, "Baby, is this another one of your tricks to try to get me to move up there with you?"

Karen simply shook her head before speaking. "No, K, please listen to what I'm saying. The place is a goldmine and you can do much better with less risk," she paused for a moment before adding, "You can make three or even four times what you make down here without sticking your neck out there like you do down here."

That got KD's attention. "And how do you know that?" He asked.

"I've seen it with my own eyes, K. A few of my classmates have been doing it to get them through, and you know I'm not too fond of that but they're making it."

"Okay, I'll think about it," said KD before returning to his food.

"Please, K. Just think about it," Karen said as she returned to her own plate.

KD convinced Karen to stay with him for another day and she agreed. After breakfast, KD contacted Dolla and Poundz on a conference call. The three all agreed to meet at Dolla's apartment to discuss some issues. While Karen loaded the dirty dishes into the dishwasher, KD rolled another spliff. Together, he and Karen took turns puffing on the spliff until there was no more left. KD gave Karen some money to go shopping afterwards, and dropped her off at her cousin's house before heading to Dolla's apartment.

Chapter 13: THE FAM

KD made it to Dolla's apartment before Poundz, as usual. Before he could knock, Dolla opened the door with a Heineken in hand. KD entered the apartment and watched Dolla shut and lock the door behind him. The strong stench of weed invaded his nostrils as he followed Dolla into his living room. Dolla's favorite album, Styles P's *A Gangsta and a Gentleman* played through the living room's speakers. Before KD could even get comfortable, "They're in the fridge," Dolla said, handing him the spliff.

KD puffed away on the spliff as he made his way to Dolla's kitchen to get himself a beer. The two sat in Dolla's living room, smoking and drinking until Poundz arrived.

"What's the big emergency, boss?" Poundz asked sarcastically as he gave the two dap.

He didn't need an invitation to fetch himself a beer from Dolla's fridge.

"Ain't no emergency and I ain't your fucking boss!" KD countered quickly not giving Poundz room to start his bullshit.

Dolla sat in silence, twisting a spliff and bobbing his head to Jadakiss and Styles P's *I'm a Ruff Ryder* track. Just like they've done over the years, the three smoked like Rasta men while discussing what was going on in their individual lives. The occasional jokes on each other brought in the laughs. Indeed, these three young men were the epitome of a dream team, considering how tight they've stuck together over the years.

After sometime of shooting the shit, KD finally decided to break the news to them by saying, "I got some news to discuss with y'all."

To make sure he had their attention, he left the floor open so they could get all the smart comments out of the way before getting down to actual business. What they were about to discuss was a serious matter, one that could change their lives for the better. KD needed everyone's undivided attention. When no one said a word for a while, he took it as his cue to start.

"Check it, Karen revealed something to me last night that I think y'all should know," he paused to see their reactions.

Dolla and Poundz both seemed to be all ears so he continued, "This can actually be good for our family," again he paused to let the suspense build up while thinking of the best way to break the news to them.

"Let's hear it, K. Why are you speaking in riddles?" Dolla asked.

KD knew then that he had their undivided attention. "According to Karen, the small town upstate where she goes to school is a goldmine waiting to be tapped into," He paused to observe their reactions.

The two nodded their heads so he continued. "Yams go for double or triple what we get down here, and this shit moves like hot cakes. We can move more yams up there in a week than we do down here, while making double or even triple the money with less risks." Again, he paused for their reactions.

"See, I knew you were a sucker for love. She popped that pussy on you and fed you that bullshit and you ran with it," said Poundz jokingly as he laughed.

"Let him finish speaking, fam!" Dolla snapped.

"Well, it wouldn't be right if you didn't look at it that way, homie," KD said calmly before adding, "This could be a big break for us." Poundz clearly struck a nerve with his comment but KD wasn't giving him that satisfaction.

"You're right, fam, this shit sounds like an opportunity. A way for us to expand our operation beyond the city limits," Poundz stated as if a lightbulb just went on in his head.

"Thank you, homie!" KD exclaimed, excited Poundz saw the situation for what it was. After watching them nod in agreement, he added, "That's what I've been telling y'all from jump. If the situation is as sweet as she claims, then we have an opportunity, but in order to know how real it is, we have to do our own footwork. We definitely can't move on her word. The floor is open for suggestions."

"Well, since she's your woman and all, why don't you go camp out with her for a week or two and test the waters, K?" Dolla suggested.

Before KD could even respond, Poundz piped in, "Nah, I'll go for as long as needed. I need some time away from the city anyhow."

KD locked eyes with Dolla for a moment, "Any objections, Dolla?"

"Fine by me," answered Dolla with a shrug.

"That's what it is then. She's headed back tomorrow night so be ready to go," KD stated more to Poundz.

Poundz and Dolla both nodded in agreement.

"Any questions, concerns, smart-ass-comments, anything?" KD asked in a sarcastic tone.

"Nothing from me," said Dolla.

"Nothing here!" Poundz chimed in.

"Say no more. We gotta put together a care package for you first thing in the morning," KD suggested and they all agreed.

For the next few hours, the three listened to music, cracked jokes, drank Heinekens, and smoked spliffs while playing video games.

It was dark when KD finally left Dolla's apartment that evening. He picked up Karen from her cousin's house then drove straight to a liquor store where he picked up three bottles of wine for his mom. Karen talked his head off about her shopping experience the entire time, which he pretended to be listening. Deep down, his mind was preoccupied with the discussion he had with his brothers.

From the liquor store, KD drove to his mom's house. It was evident his mom was happy to see them from the way she showered them with hugs, kisses, and compliments. Mom, as they've grown to call Ms. Gladys, encouraged Karen to continue pursuing her nursing degree. As they made female talk, KD carried the wine into the kitchen, where he placed them on the countertop with ten one-hundred-dollar bills underneath it. That was about the only way for him to give Mom money. She refused to take money from out of KD's hands, always claiming that he needed it more than her.

When it was time to leave, Mom insisted that they take a bowl of jerk chicken and rice with them, which they agreed, knowing they weren't getting away without it.

"Black is taking me to AC later," Mom said to KD as they exchanged goodbye hugs and kisses.

"Have fun and give Black my love, Mom," KD said in return.

"I'm so proud of you for settling down with such a beautiful young lady," Mom expressed to KD while handing him the bowl of food.

"Bye, Mom, and thanks for the food," KD said in response.

"Take good care of my boy," Mom said to Karen.

"I will, Mom," Karen responded as they walked out of the door.

KD disliked when Mom acted as if he was still a little boy but to Mom, he'd always be her little boy. They drove back to KD's apartment. Against his argument, Karen insisted on preparing them a late dinner. They both changed into comfortable attire, KD's just sweatpants and a tank top and Karen's a little skimpier and sexier — booty shorts and tank top. KD retired to the sofa to watch *The Godfather*, the old mob movie, while Karen prepared dinner.

Personally, KD preferred old classic movies to the watered-down commercial releases of the new generation. Dinner was delicious — baked chicken with homemade macaroni and cheese, and cheesecake for dessert. Over dinner, KD brought Karen up to speed regarding their plan to send Poundz with her to test the waters. She was supportive of it. KD loved Karen for her down to earth attitude.

After dinner, Karen joined KD in the living room with some wine as they finished *The Godfather*. It was romantic in a way, the two of them having drinks and enjoying a movie under candle light. Induced by a mixture of alcohol and weed, they melted into each other, falling asleep right on the living room sofa.

Chapter 14: POUNDZ

At ten after six the next evening, Karen hit the highway with Poundz in her car. Bebe followed a few car-lengths behind with Poundz's care package. For five-hundred dollars, Bebe agreed to take the trip behind them with a teddy bear full of drugs. After driving for about four hours with one pit stop for gas, the three made a safe entry into the city of Brownville around midnight.

Upon arrival, Poundz's first move was to find a spot to stash the teddy bear and his gun. Sunshine Inn, a hole-in-the-wall motel fit the bill perfectly at forty bucks a night. Bebe spent the night at Karen's apartment, and returned to the city the next day. Poundz, on the other hand, stayed up all night bagging up the drugs to get things ready.

He'd finally laid down for a catnap at the motel when he heard a knock on his room door.

"Housekeeping!" A female voice accompanied a second knock. Poundz decided to step out and grab a bite at a neighboring diner while his room was cleaned. At the diner, he ordered a cheese omelet with turkey bacon and toast. Feeling out of place, he played with his phone as he waited for his food. When his food was finally delivered, he dug right into it as if he'd been starving for days.

He'd been itching to get back to his room the entire time. For obvious reasons, the housekeeper being in his room with his teddy bear did not sit right with him. After his meal, he quickly retreated to his room. Luckily, everything was still intact just as he'd left it. Poundz smoked a spliff to the face and decided to get some sleep while he waited for Karen to pick him up.

About four hours later, he was awakened by a familiar knock. Wiping sleep out of his eyes, he checked the peephole and unlocked his room door for Karen. Karen watched television while she waited for Poundz to shower and get himself ready. The two were on their way out about a half an hour later. As they sat in Karen's car in the motel parking lot, she made some calls on her cell. That was all it took to jumpstart things for Poundz. Karen drove Poundz to a number of apartments and introduced him to people as her brother.

Poundz, moving with purpose dished out samples and his cell number to some of the people he met. He even made a number of sales in the process. As the two got back on the road, Poundz thought, *a few quick licks for $500, not bad at all.* It was sometime after six in the evening when they finally arrived at Karen's apartment. The two ordered Chinese food for dinner and lounged about for the remainder of the evening. Karen gave Poundz spare keys to both her car and apartment and advised him to feel at home.

Little by little, Poundz built a buzz for himself as the days passed. While Poundz appeared unsatisfied with the pace at which things were moving, Karen urged him to be patient and wait for the weekend. Wednesday night, Karen decided to invite Poundz to the bar where she worked as a bartender. She wasn't working on this particular night but she was destined to introduce Poundz to more people, especially her coworkers.

Al, the bar's owner whom Poundz met the night before, was happy to see him again. Karen introduced Poundz to Lisa and Joy, the other bartenders, as well as Dave, Rich, Chris, Charlie, and Mike, the bouncers. They all treated Poundz like family and in return, Poundz handed them samples. Turned out that Al and his bouncers loved to party. "That's some good stuff, you got more with you?" The questions came from left and right. Poundz knew then that things were about to change.

As the night went on, Poundz made some money and mingled with the crowd. He met Angel, a shapely blonde who took a quick liking to him. Angel was in her late twenties with no man or kids. She worked as a car salesperson with her own house and an SUV. Poundz saw that as an opportunity and spent most of the night getting to know her. By the time the bar closed, Poundz made nearly fifteen-hundred dollars, most of which came from Al and his workers.

The town was now starting to look every bit as Karen had described it to be. With the exception of two-hundred dollars, Poundz gave all the money to Karen to add to the stash before leaving the bar with Angel. From the bar, Poundz and Angel grabbed a bite at a twenty-four hour diner, then off to Angel's house, where they sexed it up into the early morning. Poundz was certain after that night that white girls were some of the freakiest females on Earth.

The weekend came and went, bringing Poundz an increased flow of clientele and money. The word circulated about how good Poundz's product was. Poundz learned the small town inside and out over a short period of time. With some help from Karen and a few of the people he'd met, Poundz knew where to and not to go, as well as most of the major players in the town. Occasionally, he'd run a name by Karen or Angel before deciding whether or not to deal with an individual.

Things gradually moved according to plan but it got better when Angel introduced Poundz to her cousin, Bob. Bob was major in the small town and seemed to know everybody. While Bob used here and there, his steady clientele made him valuable. Poundz and Bob quickly developed a bond and before long, Bob was hitting licks for Poundz.

Within a week of dealing with Bob, Poundz was in a great position. The *Rockstar* stamp Poundz represented became a thing to die for.

Poundz kept up with the flow of things, alternating his residence between Angel's and Karen's. He kept the stash on the move from motel to motel as well. Poundz stayed away from all the hot spots and questionable individuals he'd been warned about, and handled nearly all his licks through Bob. After nearly a month in Brownville, Poundz was low on product. On the Sunday of his fourth weekend, he returned to the city for a re-up. Inside a small duffle bag, which he held on to for dear life was over thirty-five-thousand dollars in cash. Indeed, Brownville proved to be everything Karen described it to be.

Chapter 15: TOUCHDOWN

Upon returning home, the first thing on Poundz's agenda was to get together with his brothers. He couldn't wait to see them, and most importantly, share his findings with them regarding Brownville. He started his morning off with a delicious breakfast with Trisha, his girlfriend, after spending the night together. After his meal, he phoned his brothers on a conference call and the three decided to get together. Considering Poundz had been on the road, KD and Dolla decided to extend him the courtesy and meet at Poundz's apartment.

It was about half past eleven when they arrived at the apartment. With the extra key Poundz gave Dolla, they had no problem entering the apartment. Following the sounds of the television to the living room, they found Poundz relaxing comfortably on his living room sofa. Since they had yet to spend time away from one another, it was a memorable moment in their young lives.

KD started with the slick talk as they exchanged

daps. "Look who found his way back home," he said tapping Dolla on the forearm.

The two busted out laughing before Dolla added, "Word, I thought I was gonna have to come get you, b."

"Muthafuckas got jokes," Poundz simply said as he joined his brothers in laughter.

The excitement level among the three was immeasurable at that particular moment. They spent some time cracking jokes on each other until Poundz strolled off in the direction of his bedroom. He returned with a black duffle bag in hand. There was a sudden quietness. Poundz simply sat down and unzipped the duffle bag.

He then said, "My brothers, this here is thirty-seven-thousand–eight-hundred big ones."

KD and Dolla both looked at the stacks of rubber-banded bills in awe. A simple experiment looked every bit like a win. KD was the first to speak as he examined the money inside the duffle bag. "Yo, you really laid it down out there, huh, P?" He asked.

While Poundz remained silent, Dolla simply said, "Word, baby bro, you made me proud," as he stared at the bag full of money. Dolla put the finishing touches on the spliff he'd been rolling. When Poundz finally ended his silence, he struck something deep within the two of them. "Ain't no slouches in this family, homie!" He said with conviction.

"Facts!" That was all KD said before extending his right fist to Poundz.

Poundz bumped fists with KD and they held the contact for a moment. Just then, Dolla lit the spliff and joined the two with his fist. "One for all, and all for one!" The trio said in unison.

The trio passed the spliff among themselves as they counted every bill that was in the duffle bag. As expected, they arrived exactly at thirty-seven-thousand-eight-hundred dollars. Afterwards, Poundz told KD and Dolla exactly what he'd done in Brownville to get up to that point, and how he'd done it. Without a doubt, Brownville could become a major addition to their operation. What really sealed things off was when Poundz assured KD and Dolla that he'd be headed back to Brownville in exactly one week.

Chapter 16: THE EXODUS

After meeting up with his brothers, Poundz decided to make good use of his time. He spent the next few days getting his affairs in order, which consisted mostly of spending time with Trisha and convincing her not to worry about him too much. It was now time to make the move to Brownville permanently and Poundz was up for the task. Poundz understood that he was about to make a major sacrifice but when it came to the family, there were no limits to how far they would go.

On the evening of his seventh day, Poundz loaded the trunk of his Chevy with a suitcase of clothing and drove to the stash house, where KD and Dolla awaited.

"You ready to make this move, baby bro?" Asked Dolla, the moment Poundz walked in the door.

"Born ready, baby!" Shot back Poundz confidently as they exchanged dap.

"That's what I like to hear," KD chimed in.

The three sat for a moment, chatting among themselves. They ironed out the contents of Poundz's package this time around, as well as what to expect back. They also went over the plan for the Brownville move. It was a simple one — Poundz would go in and establish a strong presence. He'd recruit some local soldiers as he saw fit. If needed, they would send their own soldiers up from the city.

The goal was to go after both the retail and wholesale drug markets of Brownville. Just as she'd done the first time, Bebe was ready to follow behind with the package for double the fee. The three brothers understood that Poundz was taking a much bigger package this time, and that they had a lot riding on this particular trip. Should things go well, then they would officially add Brownville to their operation. If not, then they would just see it for what it was worth.

It was about seven o'clock in the evening when Poundz decided to leave the city. With fewer cars on the road at night, he and Bebe were likely to get there quicker and safer. After exchanging daps with his brothers, he hit the road. Bebe followed a few minutes later as promised. They would meet back up at a prearranged location and fuel up before hitting the highway.

Chapter 17: ROTATION

Days turned into weeks, and weeks into months in Brownville. Poundz gradually but strategically established the foundation for their operation. During his second flip, he managed to recruit a handful of reliable local soldiers and independent hustlers. He also expanded their reach on both the retail and wholesale avenues. Three soldiers from the city were also sent up to strengthen Poundz's camp.

Brownville officially became a major part of their operation with growth possibilities. The earning potential clearly exceeded twice that of their city operation. It was a matter of expansion and longevity at this point, which was a major element in the drug game. They understood that with the right management, Brownville could easily provide them the longevity that they hoped.

Hell, they only had two flips and the turnout had been nothing short of extraordinary. With both their city and Brownville operations combined, they couldn't ask for a better position to be in. Yet, they remained humble, not letting the fast money overshadow their vision. They were determined to succeed in the game, and by succeed: to get filthy rich, and live large while staying alive and free.

Their focus now lay on building upon the foundation that they had established. When Poundz was gearing up for his third flip, the idea was birthed. They decided to take turns overseeing the Brownville operation to give them each a fair break away from the fast-paced city life. It was a simple idea but a very effective one. Not only would they be making full use of their available resources, but they would also keep the family leveled.

After toying with the idea for some time, KD decided to be the next to test the Brownville waters. Being that his precious Karen resided in Brownville, KD saw an opportunity to kill two birds with one stone. Not only would he be able to spend a substantial amount of time with her, but he'd also be useful to the family at the same time. Dolla would relieve him when his turn came but for the time being, he'd have to oversee their city operation single-handedly until Poundz returned.

This, of course depended on how long it would take KD to settle into Brownville. Dolla was willing and able to oversee things until Poundz returned home. The trio sat down with Black and disclosed their plans to him, which he approved. Actually, Black had grown proud of them for what they had accomplished over such a short period.

Their bond with Black now was much stronger than

the initial stages. Anything they ever needed, be it advice, product, manpower, machinery or influence, Black was able and willing to provide. The three young men were living the life that they envisioned and dreamed. Black, having granted them his full backing, was more like nurturing to him. After all, he needed someone levelheaded enough to replace him when time came for him to step down or retire from the game.

On the day that Poundz was scheduled to return to Brownville, KD joined him. They each drove in their own vehicle. As usual, Bebe made sure that their package arrived safely. With Angel and Karen in town, KD and Poundz's living arrangements were well taken care of. It hadn't taken but a week for KD to get the hang of things in Brownville. Poundz decided to stay with him a few more days to make sure things ran smoothly.

The two spent a total of a week and a half together in Brownville. While it was a total change of pace and territory for KD, the goal remained the same. He made the necessary adjustments and in no time, things were running as smooth as butter under his leadership. Poundz returned to the city to join Dolla, feeling very confident and with a sense of pride. Deep down inside, he not only knew but he felt that their Brownville operation was in great hands.

Before long, Dolla's turn arrived. They were closing in on their first year in Brownville and their operation had been on a constant rise. The four months that KD spent in

Brownville went by nearly unnoticed. Just as Poundz did with him, KD brought Dolla to Brownville with him on his next flip. He also brought two more soldiers with them to help strengthen their camp.

Showing Dolla the ropes took about two weeks, after which KD returned to the city to join Poundz. The trio kept their rotation in effect, raking in a substantial amount of money from their operation. They had even gone as far as spreading their reach further beyond the Brownville limits. They saw a market in dire need and being the opportunists that they were; they quickly took advantage and fulfilled it.

Chapter 18: MAN DOWN

KD had just returned to the city after spending some time with the Brownville team. Their presence was as concrete as could be and they were all in full appreciation of it. Taking in nearly ninety percent of Brownville's drug supply was just a scratch on the surface. What started as a simple experiment turned into a major operation, bringing in loads and loads of cash week after week. No regrets there.

Even Black commended them on their movements at one point, considering the amount of product they were taking from him at any given time. This was not only great for their young egos but it boosted their confidence as well. Receiving a commendation from a man of Black's stature, a true legend, was not an everyday thing. Indeed, they deserved to feel good about themselves.

On a hot summer afternoon, KD set his air conditioner to high. It was the day following his return to the city. He was sitting in his apartment, re-counting the money he just brought home when his phone rang. Dolla's number appeared across the screen.

"Yo," he picked up.

"Yo, what's goodie?" Asked Dolla.

"Ain't shit, what's goodie with you?"

"I'm getting Chinese, whatchu want?"

"Get me my regular wings with shrimp fried rice." KD said then hung up.

He returned his attention to the money. When he finished re-counting it, he zipped up the military-style duffle bag that the money was in and tossed it underneath the coffee table. The doorbell rung shortly thereafter, it was Dolla. He let Dolla in the apartment before proceeding to the bathroom to wash his hands. The smell of Chinese food invaded KD's nostrils upon his return from the bathroom. Dolla was already fist deep in his beef and broccoli platter at the dining table. A half-consumed bottle of Guinness sat to his right.

"Guinness in the fridge," said Dolla, pointing at the bag of Chinese food.

KD fetched himself a Guinness from the fridge, opened it, and took a swig. He then joined Dolla at the dining table, tearing right into his own plate of Chinese food. The two ate in silence and watched ESPN on the small dining room television. The analysts were discussing Plaxico

Burress' possible return to the New York Giants or maybe the Pittsburgh Steelers.

As a devout Giants fan, KD hoped he'd return to the team. After all, he'd caught the winning touchdown in their Super Bowl win over the New England Patriots. After eating, they smoked some haze that Dolla brought and discussed what had been going on the last few months. Things were going as smooth as expected on both ends with the exception of a few minor issues, nothing worth worrying about.

The two re-counted the money KD brought home before adding it to what they had in KD's big safe. Being away from the city for so long had KD itching to get into something. The two made plans to check out Stars, a new nightclub in Harlem. They agreed to meet back up at KD's apartment around eleven and head to the club. Of course, KD hit Dolla for some of that haze before he left his apartment.

After Dolla left, KD called Black to let him know he was back in the city. Black suggested that they have breakfast the next morning and catch up on things; KD agreed before hanging up. He decided to catch a quick nap in anticipation of the night ahead of them. That only lasted two hours. KD lounged around until he realized it was past eight in the evening. He couldn't believe how late in the day it was.

He finally got out of bed and loaded Jay-z's *Volume 3* album into his living room stereo system, keeping the volume at medium level. He then took a long relaxing shower. Afterwards, he went to the closet to select an outfit for the night — black True Religion jeans with a black button down — something casual. He rolled himself a spliff of haze and smoked before getting dressed. While he waited for Dolla, he pre-rolled five spliffs for the night.

Just as planned, Dolla called around a quarter till eleven and said he was on his way over. The black Louie Vuitton loafers gave KD's outfit a sense of class. A splash of Joop Jump and his big chain with the diamond encrusted cross pendant and diamond encrusted pinky ring was all he needed. The big-faced Breitling watch on his left wrist complemented his jewelry to perfection. One last look at himself in his dresser mirror assured him he was ready to go.

When Dolla called and said he was downstairs, KD simply tucked his pistol in his waistband, grabbed his phone, keys, case of pre-rolled spliffs and out the door he went. They shared a spliff on the short drive down the West Side Highway to the club.

The place was new alright — the new hot spot. The line to get in went way down the block. The ratio had to be about four to one, female to male. It was a big night with the rap duo Mobb Deep scheduled to perform sometime after midnight. Despite the long line, a one-hundred-dollar bill to Bully, one of the club's bouncers whom Dolla knew got them ushered right to VIP. A group of females who claimed to be their *friends* were also ushered in with them.

The four females went on their way upon entering the club and KD couldn't be more grateful. All he wanted to do was have fun and enjoy himself. The place was alive indeed, as they watched the crowd gradually grow by the minute.

Waitresses brought bottles of Hennessy and Belaire Rose to them upon paying for their VIP section. The DJ really knew how to rock the crowd as he played some of the Infamous' classic tracks — *Shook Ones, Quiet Storm, The Getaway...*

The DJ had the crowd in a frenzy, a sure sign that they were ready for the Mobb's performance. The drinks flowed and so did the spliffs. For a while, KD and Dolla played the cut until three very good-looking females followed the smell of haze right to their section.

"Hi, I'm Sonya! You mind if we join you guys?" A sexy mixed female in a black party dress asked.

Dolla examined the three females for a moment before waving them over.

"This is Monica and Jeannette," Sonya introduced her girlfriends.

"What's goodie, y'all? I'm Dolla Bill and this is my man K," Dolla said to them in response.

"Nice to meet you guys." Monica and Jeannette said in unison.

"Thanks for letting us join you, it's so packed in here tonight," added Sonya.

KD and Dolla weren't in the mood for all that chit-chat so they spread the spliff and bubbly to keep the chatting at a minimum. The ladies kept them company and in return, they kept the spliffs in rotation and the bubbly flowing. When Havoc and Prodigy took the stage at 1:30 a.m., the crowd went berserk. The Mobb performed classic after classic, including *Shook Ones, Quiet Storm, and The Getaway.*

As the festivities continued, competition amongst their female companions became obvious. Each one tried their hardest to capture their attention. One after the other, they danced and showed what they could do with their curves. KD took a liking to Jeannette and it was obvious that Dolla was feeling Sonya from the way he looked at her. However, KD and Dolla were quick to let it be known that they didn't play favoritism. They were willing to get to know all three of them, possibly at the same place and at the same time.

It was after three when KD checked the time. The place was still alive. The Mobb's performance had only lasted about an hour but the DJ kept the crowd moving. A few scuffles broke out on the dance floor but the bouncers had been on their jobs, restoring order right away. At three-thirty, KD hinted to Dolla about leaving. He definitely wasn't trying to be caught up with the rest of the crowd at closing time.

Their female companions didn't like the idea so Dolla invited them to an after party, which they agreed. Numbers were exchanged before KD and Dolla paid their tab and left a healthy tip for the waitress. Bully made his way to their section and led them out of the club with no problem. The fresh air felt great on their skin outside.

With Dolla's Escalade parked a block away, the pair started making their way towards the SUV. They rounded the first corner and were almost at their destination when KD spotted a man dressed in dark clothing approaching from the opposite direction. Initially, he shrugged off any suspicions, thinking it was just a fellow club-goer. It wasn't until they were mere feet from the man that they saw the gun.

Off their normal game, they had been so relaxed in the club atmosphere that, though they were both strapped, they had no time to react.

"Let's do this the easy way, hand over the ice!" The gunman instructed, pointing his gun at KD.

Was this because he was wearing the bigger chain? They would have to figure that out later, but for now, their safeties were their main concerns. Both men raised their hands in surrender.

"Dammit, man!" Dolla cussed out his mouth.

Quickly and quietly, KD replayed the night in his head. Nothing suspicious besides the females, both the *friends* crew and good-looking crew. Either crew could have been in cahoots with this gunman but how could they find out?

"Fuck!" KD cussed under his breath.

"Hurry the fuck up before I squeeze off!" Gunman barked with a serious tone this time.

Dolla glanced at KD and he nodded, saying, "Give it to him, homie."

Slowly, they both peeled off their jewelry and handed them to the gunman one at a time. Earrings, rings, bracelets, KD watched on mad as the gunman pocketed their charm. A slight smile appeared on the gunman's face as he pocketed the jewelry, which told KD he'd let his guard down.

"We've got to use this to our advantage." KD thought to himself.

Dolla looked at KD as he undid his watch. That Cartier had been his favorite watch for as long as KD could remember and the hurt was evident on Dolla's face as he watched him hand it to the robber. Hell, he'd invested nearly fifteen-thousand dollars into that watch. KD nodded twice and gave Dolla an eye signal.

"Give me your fucking chains!" The gunman barked as he took Dolla's watch.

KD handed the gunman his own Breitling watch and proceeded to remove his chain. When Dolla handed the gunman his chain, KD watched the gunman's eyes drop to inspect the heavy chain in his hand.

Advantage!

KD made his move. He swung his chain with all his might, catching the gunman in his face with its heavy pendant. The gunman staggered backwards, letting off a wild shot.

The shot could have been accidental but there was no time to analyze because KD was on the pavement, clutching his abdomen.

"Son of a bitch!" KD cussed.

Three more shots rang out, "Die, muthafucka! Die, muthafucka! Die!" Dolla barked, followed by two more shots.

Dolla said something to KD but he didn't fully comprehend.

"I finished the fool, fam! How bad he hit you?" Dolla asked as he crouched next to KD and examined his wound.

"Not too bad, I should be good." KD responded.

"You're losing a lot of blood; we gotta get you out of here," Dolla said to KD before screaming to the gathering crowd, "call the ambulance, somebody!"

"Here, take this," KD said, handing Dolla his chain before adding, "Get the rest!"

KD watched as Dolla emptied the gunman's pockets into his own.

"Help me up, son." KD called to Dolla.

Once KD was up, he gripped his own gun and squeezed two shots into the gunman's dead body. Club-goers filled the sidewalk as if there was some kind of show going on. As KD stood, gun in hand, ready to empty his clip into the dead gunman's face, he saw a man dressed similar to the dead man moving in their direction with a pistol in his hand.

Without hesitation, KD squeezed off two wild shots in the man's direction. The man ducked behind a car but Dolla was on him, squeezing shot after shot. KD watched this second man's body jerk this way, then that as the bullets struck him. When the man finally dropped to the pavement, Dolla walked over and took his gun from him. Just like KD contemplated doing to the first gunman, Dolla squeezed off a few shots into the man's face, leaving him a mess.

"Call the ambulance, somebody!" Dolla barked at the crowd once again before walking to the first gunman and doing to him what he'd done to his partner.

They heard sirens from afar. Dolla walked to where KD was leaning against a car and said, "Hold on, man, the ambulance is coming." He then looked at the crowd and barked, "Call the fucking ambulance!"

KD began to feel light-headed from the blood loss.

"Here, take the guns and go, son." He managed to whisper.

"Nah, I ain't leaving you! I ain't fucking leaving you, man!" Dolla responded.

The sirens grew louder, the ambulance? No, the cops? Maybe both?

"The cops! Just go, tell my..." Were KD's last words before he went unconscious.

Chapter 19: SCRUBS

KD woke up feeling groggy in a room full of noisy machines. From the size of the bed he laid in alone, he knew he wasn't at his apartment. He looked to his left and met a bedrail, then a curtain. He looked to his right, same thing. Up above was a ceiling with an unfamiliar pattern. He squeezed his eyes shut momentarily and reopened them wider, hoping for a better view. Nothing changed. *Where am I?* He wondered.

He attempted to rub his eyes with his hands, and he saw it all: the numerous tubes connected to his body, sending him fluids and oxygen. The humming and beeping sounds from the machines around him, that distinct smell and that weird music that played from up above told him he was at some kind of health facility.

"What the fuck?" He muttered as he wondered which facility he was at and why he was there in the first place.

He attempted to move his body and felt an

excruciating pain in his abdominal area.

"Ouch," he muttered again.

His entire body ached like hell, yet he mustered enough energy to move the blankets off him. The bloody bandages turned his stomach but it was the blood-stained bedsheets that scared him the most. He heard a sudden change of tone in the beeping of one of the machines. Footsteps quickly approached.

The curtains parted open, making way for a number of medical workers. Nurses, dressed in scrubs of different colors and patterns soon surrounded him. Some attended to the machines while the rest attended to him and the fluids that were connected to him. *Where had these people come from so quickly?* He wondered.

"How are you feeling, my dear?" A female voice asked.

KD simply lied there, blinking his eyes. He attempted to speak, to get some answers to his many questions. He opened his mouth to speak but the words just wouldn't come out. He lied there helplessly, listening to the nurses and their health mumbo-jumbo.

"Don't stress yourself, dear. Everything will be fine," a middle-aged brown-skinned woman said, leaning in to look at KD's face.

KD nodded his head in response.

"Are you in pain, dear?" The middle-aged lady asked and KD nodded again.

"The Lord wasn't ready for you yet, the bullet went in and out," said the middle-aged lady as she adjusted the fluids.

KD's look changed to that of confusion. *Who is this lady and what is she talking about?* He wondered as he squinted his eyes. He attempted to speak again but nothing came out. Just then, he felt his eyelids beginning to get heavier.

"Just relax; rest up and let the medication do its job," the middle-aged lady said, but KD was drifting slowly off to sleep. He attempted to blink his heavy eyelids but the pain medications pumping through his veins overpowered him. The last thing he felt as he fell asleep was his blankets being pulled up to his chest.

Chapter 20: GINGERBREAD MAN

Dolla stepped out of the shower and turned his attention to his still ringing cellphone. With a towel wrapped around his waist, he studied the unknown number on the screen, wondering who was blowing up his phone. His initial thought was KD or Black but that thought soon vanished after seeing the 914 area code. Puzzled, he waited for the voicemail alert and dialed one to listen. Upon hearing KD's voice, he nearly dropped the phone out of sheer shock.

The new voicemail message played, "Yo son, I just got done talking to the d's. I'm going to The Island whenever I get discharged. They got me cuffed to my bed now. Shit is real but you know what to do, one luv!"

Dolla stared at his phone dumbfounded. He played the message a second, then a third time before he was able to process the message. Hanging up the phone, he rushed to his bedroom to get dressed. Once dressed, he packed himself a duffle bag of clothes and emptied the contents of his safe into another bag. He hauled both bags downstairs and loaded them into the trunk of his new Audi A8.

He ran back upstairs to make sure his apartment was secured before getting on the move. As Dolla drove away, he kept a constant eye in the rearview mirror to make sure he wasn't followed. The news he just received brought on a sudden change of plans for him. Dolla drove to KD's apartment, making a number of detours to make sure he hadn't attracted any unwanted company.

Upon arrival, he tossed the entire duffle bag containing the contents of his safe into KD's big black safe. Just as he was about to lock the safe up, his phone rang again startling the life out of him. He was relieved to see Black's number on the screen. "What's up, Unk?" He quickly answered.

"What's up, nephew? Is everything alright?" Black asked from the other end.

"I'm cool, Unk. How you been?" Dolla asked in response.

"Good, good. Come up to the joint, we got some work to do there," Black simply said then hung up.

Dolla returned to locking up the safe. He took one last look around KD's apartment before locking the front door and heading back downstairs. The drive to the nightclub took Dolla about forty-five minutes. Again, he'd taken a number of detours to make sure he wasn't followed.

Upon arrival, he parked in the staff parking area and walked to the back door where Black awaited him.

"How you holding up, nephew?" Black asked as the two shook hands and walked inside the building.

The stress on Dolla's face was evident, and he had every right to be. He was a wanted man in connection with a double homicide investigation.

"I'm still alive, Unk. And that's all that matters," responded Dolla casually as he tried to hide the stress on his face.

"What's new? You got anything new?" Black asked.

"K just left me a message earlier, that's about it." Dolla said then continued to share the contents of the voicemail with Black.

Black reciprocated by sharing the news he'd discovered during his last visit with KD. While it was unlike Black to interfere with his nephews' dealings, this was one exception. The young ones needed him and he was willing to be there for them. They needed his guidance more than anything, and he was prepared to rise to the occasion. Black and Dolla devised a quick emergency plan, and then shared a spliff before parting ways.

Chapter 21: CHANGEUP

From Black's club, Dolla hit the highway on an impromptu visit with Poundz and the Brownville team. For the interim, Cash would operate independently but not for long. The drive to Brownville took Dolla longer than usual. He was tired, yet he took his time on the road, knowing his situation. Having traded his Audi for Black's C-class Mercedes, along with a new identity, he was determined to make the most out of his situation.

He had more than enough cash to hold him down for a few months. Upon arrival, Dolla checked himself into a local Holiday Inn right off the highway to get some rest. With his new identity, he had no problem securing a room for three nights. Settled now, he called Poundz but got his voicemail. He called a second time and got the same result, so he decided to leave him a message. This was clearly not the response he expected at a time like this.

To calm his nerves, Dolla rolled himself a spliff and lit it as he got ready to shower. He contemplated his next move as he stood in front of the bathroom mirror, puffing on the spliff. He was halfway through his spliff, when his cellphone buzzed. "Yo," he answered after seeing his brother's number come across the screen.

"Yo, what's goodie, homie?" Poundz inquired from the other end.

"Ain't shit, what's good, baby-bro?"

"You still around?"

"All day!"

"Say no more, here I come," Poundz said then hung up.

Dolla decided to scratch the shower idea since he didn't know how long his brother would take to get there. About ten minutes went by, no sign of Poundz. Ten more minutes later, a familiar sound rattled on the door. Although Dolla knew that knock all too well from using it since childhood, he failed to let his guard down. "Who is it?" He asked.

"Open up!" Poundz barely finished before the door cracked open.

He stepped inside, locking the door behind him. "My man, fifty grand!" Poundz called as the two embraced in a brief manly hug.

"How is life treating you, bro?" Dolla inquired.

"Can't complain 'cause ain't nobody gon' listen anyway," Poundz answered before asking, "What brings you up this way?"

"Take a load off, man. What's the rush?" Dolla asked, turning the volume up on the television.

Poundz heeded his big brother's advice and seated himself on the corner of the king-sized bed. Dolla took a few more pulls before passing the spliff to Poundz.

"How's K?" Poundz asked as he took the spliff.

"You don't wanna know, fam," Dolla answered before adding, "Shit is twisted to the t!"

"Damn, shit is that bad?" Poundz pressed on.

"Remember that shit I told you happened outside the club?"

Poundz nodded, passing the spliff back to Dolla, who took two quick pulls and said, "Well, shit hit the fan and now I gotta duck. They got K chained to his bed at the hospital, talking about The Island," Dolla passed the spliff back to Poundz before adding, "Shit is fucked up, son!"

"Hold up. I thought K was the one who got hit?" Poundz asked puzzled.

"Yea, but what I didn't tell you was that we left two cats stinking that night." Dolla continued to give his baby brother the extended version of what transpired at the club that night. Poundz nodded in understanding by the time

Dolla finished talking.

"So now, what's the game plan?" Poundz asked before adding with wide eyes, "And don't tell me our shit is over."

"Nah, baby-bro, shit is far from over." Dolla said then added, "I gotta lay low but the saga continues. Our shit is running way too smooth to just let it go."

"So what we gonna do?" Poundz asked.

"I'm here to hold shit down up here while you go run shit down bottom. That way I can lay low and still be productive." Dolla responded.

"Sounds like a plan." Poundz added, nodding his head.

"We'll talk more about this but for now we need to find a good spot to get some grub," Dolla said, rubbing his belly to emphasize his hunger.

They both laughed at Dolla's remark before heading outside. The two left the hotel in Poundz's Charger in search of a good place to eat.

Chapter 22: BAD BOY

After spending nearly two weeks recovering in the hospital, KD was released into the custody of the NYPD. Just as he'd expected, Detective Valdez and his Caucasian partner, Detective Stevens, both of whom he'd met on previous occasions, detained and transported him to the 28th Precinct in Harlem. It was a Monday morning but KD had no other plans aside from figuring out a way to get out of custody.

Upon arriving at the precinct, the detectives searched KD yet again, taking all his belongings for safekeeping. He was re-mirandized by Detective Valdez, a fair-skinned Hispanic man, who took down KD's name and other pertinent information.

He was fingerprinted afterwards. Shackled to a steel bench in a mid-sized holding cell, his hands were still handcuffed behind his back as the detectives left to run his information through their system.

As KD sat in the cold cell, he did a quick evaluation

of the situation and the possible outcomes. He knew his options were limited, and so were his chances of freedom at this moment. He had a wildcard, though, which he planned to keep in the hole until it was absolutely necessary. Black was aware of the situation and assured him not to worry, which worked in his favor as well.

Hell, knowing Black, he probably had his lawyer on the case already. It was all a matter of getting through this initial process. KD was in deep thought in the smelly cell when Detective Stevens emerged. The Caucasian man was fuming, with a pen and a pocket-sized notepad in his hand. KD didn't need a psychic to tell him that the detective was not happy about something.

"Let's try this again, ass-wipe. What's your real name and date of birth?" The detective blurted out before he made his way inside the cell. He was angry and it was obvious he was in no mood for games.

Deciding to work on his nerves, KD remained silent not even bothering to look his way, let alone answer his questions. The middle-aged detective stood a few steps away from where KD sat and repeated his question. Again, he received the same response — silence.

"You wanna fuck around?" The enraged policeman asked while staring angrily down at KD. He then added, "I have nothing but time."

KD watched Detective Stevens take a few steps backwards and for a moment, he thought the lawman was going to have a seat. Instead, he simply placed his pen and notepad on the other steel bench. KD continued to play on the lawman's nerves, not giving him the time of day.

"I see you wanna fuck around." The angry detective said and quickly closed the distance between them like a hungry beast. His steps were sharp, his hands slowly balling up into fists as he approached KD. His anger loomed over KD like a black cloud as his pale face slowly turned beet-red. KD could see a huge vein on the side of the lawman's temple as he got within striking distance. It was at that moment that KD braced himself for the unthinkable.

KD's eyes nearly closed voluntarily, but he forced them open. *Never let them see you sweat.* His uncle's words ran through his head like a nursery rhyme.

The detective raised his hand in a swinging motion and KD clenched his jaws in anticipation of the assault. Instead of a blow, however, the lawman thrust his index finger in KD's face, inches from his right eye. The lawman brought his face so close to KD's that he could smell his aftershave.

"Let me tell you something, you black son-of-a-bitch," barked the lawman through gritted teeth.

KD's own rage was building up at the sound of the lawman's racist tone.

"You wanna go around killing people and expect nothing to happen?" The lawman barked again, this time spit flew from his mouth and landed on KD's nose.

The smell of his unpleasantly stale breath, a mixture of coffee and cigarettes, was so close to KD's face that he felt like puking. KD's jaws clenched tighter and he bit down hard to release some of his anger. At that very moment, he prayed that the handcuffs would magically free his wrists. He realized the powerless position he was in. Physically, his movements were restricted to the bare minimum.

"I have all fucking day if you wanna dick around," the lawman spoke again as he rose upright and gave KD this murderous look that could've knocked down a goddamned elephant. "No matter what you do, I still get to go home and fuck my wife tonight while you sit here and eat cheese sandwiches," the lawman continued before turning to walk away, but not before adding, "I win either way."

Chapter 23: GRILL' EM

The lawman returned to the cell with his partner moments later, but this time his aggression was gone. Detective Stevens stood by the entrance to the cell while his partner approached KD. Detective Valdez spoke in a much softer tone as he approached. "Listen; there is no need in complicating things. It's only gonna prolong your stay here. The quicker you give us your real information, the quicker we can process you and get you out of here."

Something about the detective's calm and friendly tone screamed fishy. *Just a moment ago, your partner was in here trying to wring my neck and here you come with this nearly feminine approach?* KD thought to himself.

"C'mon, partner, if he wanna stay here longer then let him." Detective Stevens, obviously still boiling inside, added his piece from across the cell.

KD finally looked at the lawmen, from one to the other then spoke calmly, "I already gave you the right information. Just what else do you want from me?"

Detective Stevens made this strange throaty sound and moved quickly in KD's direction as if he was coming for blood, but his partner stopped him before he can get too close.

"Let me deal with him, partner." Detective Valdez said in an attempt to calm his enraged partner.

KD watched the angry lawman return to his previous position as his partner attempted to convince him to cooperate.

"I'm gonna ask you one last time then it is out of my hands. What are your real name, address, and date of birth?" The Detective asked.

KD looked the lawman dead in his eyes before speaking. "You just detained me from a hospital, right? Why don't you get my discharge papers out of my property and find out?" He asked calmly.

"C'mon, partner, we're done here." Detective Valdez threw his hands up in frustration as he followed his partner out of the cell. A uniformed officer entered the cell moments later and signaled for KD to follow him. He received the same treatment as Detective Valdez. The uniform walked over and yanked KD up by his shirt only to discover that he was shackled to the bench. The only thing that stopped KD from fighting back were the restraints on his ankles and wrists.

"I'll make sure my lawyer knows about all this shit," KD threatened the uniform as he was escorted out of the cell and down to what looked like an interrogation room.

The uniform, clearly not concerned with KD's threats, simply said, "Have a seat!" In this new room, five minutes turned into ten, and then twenty before Detective Valdez and another man entered the room. This new man, African-American descent, introduced himself as Detective Cobb.

"George Blackman, Jr, right?" Detective Cobb spoke first, seating himself across from KD.

KD remained silent.

"Partner, let me take these cuffs off him." Detective Cobb said more to KD than his partner. He looked at his partner for approval before unlocking and removing the silver links off KD's wrists. "Remember me, George? Detective Cobb, we met at Harlem Hospital." Said Detective Cobb.

More silence.

"Fuck that! This fucker doesn't wanna cooperate, let me get right to the point, partner," barked Detective Valdez who had been leaning against the wall off to the side.

"Well, I tried," said Detective Cobb as he stood and walked to the back of the room.

Detective Valdez placed a stack of papers on the table and seated himself across from KD. He unbuttoned his jacket and loosened up his tie before speaking. "Now you listen to me, dammit, the name you gave me was bogus and you know it. Now, I'm not a big fan of wasting time so let's try this again." Detective Valdez said with a serious tone.

"Hard to tell because y'all wasting mine," KD said sarcastically in response.

"I doubled and triple checked it and I know you didn't die and come to life."

There it was. He caught KD off guard with that one. The secret was out and KD had to find a way to counter or at least distract them until he could think of something.

"I know you didn't die in a car wreck with your mother over ten years ago. You might wanna start talking." Added Valdez.

"I don't know what the fuck you're talking about. How can I be dead if I'm sitting in front of you?" KD countered. It was a stall move but it had to work until he could think of something solid.

"So you're telling me I don't know what I'm talking about?" Detective Valdez asked, pointing to the stack of papers for emphasis.

"Shit, if you did I wouldn't be sitting here right now." Again, KD answered sarcastically.

126

For the better part of three hours, the detectives took turns peppering KD with question after question but KD stood his ground. They tried every trick in the book, but KD wouldn't budge. His responses to their questions were either smart remarks or simply, "I want my lawyer." They grew irate and threatened to call in the feds but none of that fazed KD.

Finally, out of frustration the lawmen charged KD with a number of criminal charges: murder and assault with a deadly weapon, two counts each. Of course, KD's repeated requests for food and water fell on deaf ears. After he was charged, the detectives transported KD to the Central Booking facility on 161st Street in the Bronx.

As he was escorted into the building, flanked by detectives Valdez and Stevens on the left and right sides respectively, he lifted his head just in time to see the sign from across the street. It was the sign of the Concourse Plaza Cinema, the same theater he'd taken Karen on their first date. Instantly, thoughts of his girlfriend drowned KD.

While they spoke on the phone almost every day while he was in the hospital, the thought that he may go away for a long time never occurred to him. His stomach turned at the thought of the charges he faced. He thought about running but he knew he wouldn't get far before the trigger-happy police officers gunned him down as they did Sean Bell and the others (RIP).

Against his will, he put his head down and let his legs carry him the rest of the way into the building. Inside, he went through the booking process, sticking to his story and giving the booking officer the same information he'd given the detectives. The detectives were there to tell their own version of the story, however.

Regardless, that didn't make a difference since KD made it clear that he was sticking to his story. After his fingerprints were taken for the second time, he was allowed to join the other detainees in transition to see a judge for arraignment.

Chapter 24: NO BAIL

The line to see the judge was about as long as the Great Wall of China, a problem caused by the ever-growing New York City criminal population and the understaffed justice system. From the booking floor where KD started, it took him in excess of twelve hours to make it to the first floor to see the judge for arraignment. During that time, he was among a group of about twenty detainees.

They were fed oversized cheese sandwiches and milk for lunch and dinner. Dessert came in the form of oranges tossed into the bullpen like farmers feeding their livestock. KD talked to a handful of detainees through the night, most of them headed to the county jail or *The Island* as it was popularly called. As the seconds turned into minutes, and minutes into hours, most of the detainees fell asleep on the bare bullpen floor.

KD wondered how they could even sleep with the strong stench of urine that occupied the windowless bullpen. The clock ticked, taking with it detainee after detainee. Finally, morning came and the guards began sending groups of five detainees upstairs to see the judge. KD was among the third group of detainees to be sent upstairs.

Entering the courtroom, KD prayed that the judge would give him a decent bail or bond. He wasn't surprised to see Detective Valdez seated in the back of the courtroom. When his name and case was announced, a fair-skinned female attorney stepped up to represent him. She introduced herself as Ms. Roberts from Legal Aide. KD hoped she'd be able to negotiate a decent bail amount on his behalf.

The charges were read, stirring up murmurs among the courtroom crowd. Two counts of murder among others, both of which carried twelve-year minimum prison terms. The judge spoke first. "Does the defendant have an attorney in this matter?" He asked.

Ms. Roberts cleared her throat before speaking. "Yes, your honor, I'll be representing the defendant."

The judge spoke again, this time with a bit of aggression. "Do The People oppose bail in this matter?" Asked the judge.

"Your honor, The People requests a no bail in this matter," a quick response came from the District Attorney's corner.

"Anything from the defendant, Ms. Roberts?" The

judge asked KD's attorney.

Again, Ms. Roberts cleared her throat before speaking. "Your honor, my client is a high school graduate who works as a package attendant at UPX. He was just discharged from Harlem Hospital after being treated for gunshot wounds, relating to this incident. I ask that you set bail at a considerable amount to allow him to attain full recovery at home." She said.

KD watched on as the judge listened attentively to his attorney. He wasn't sure where Ms. Roberts got her information from, but he sure wasn't complaining. She had spoken very highly of him and he appreciated every bit of it. He just hoped the judge would bite.

KD said a quick prayer as he watched the judge contemplate for a moment. The judge turned to the DA and asked, "Does the people have anything to add?"

"Yes, your honor!" The axe-faced District Attorney responded quickly before adding, "It appears that the defendant has been uncooperative since his arrest. There seem to be some red flags in his background."

"Red flags?" The judge asked with a confused grin.

"May I approach, your honor?" Asked the small female District Attorney as she glanced towards Detective Valdez in the back of the courtroom.

The judge granted the DA's request and she strolled towards the judge's bench with Ms. Roberts in tow. After a series of back and forth whispering, the lawyers returned to their positions. The judge cleared his throat then spoke up, "Ms. Roberts, it appears that your client has been uncooperative since his arrest. It also appears that your client has other legal issues, specifically with his status in the country. Considering these issues and his instant charges, I cannot grant bail at this time. No bail is my final decision!" The judge said, banging his gavel. "Next matter, please," added the judge, leaving Ms. Roberts no room to argue.

"Sorry, sir. I tried but they wouldn't go for it," Ms. Roberts turned to KD and said.

Angry, KD thought about cussing her out but after giving it a second thought, he realized that she didn't have control over the situation. He simply nodded his head before the guards hauled him out of the courtroom. As he left the courtroom, escorted by two officers, he glanced to his left just in time to see a smiling Detective Valdez make his own exit.

Back in the bullpen, KD felt nothing but disappointment and anger as he thought about the outcome of his arraignment. From the look of things, he knew he was headed to the belly of the beast for the long haul. *Fuck it; can't cry over spilled milk.* He told himself. KD was still in deep thought when a guard tossed a box of oranges into the bullpen. KD watched as the other detainees swarmed around the box like bees to honey.

Like a mad man, he got up, walked to the box, and

snatched up the last two oranges. As he returned to his spot on the steel bench, he dared someone to say something to him.

No one said a word, just mad and hungry eyes looking around. He told himself he was just warming up. They say, *when in Rome, do as the Romans do.* If he was going to be living with the wolves, then he was going to live like one.

Chapter 25: FREEDOM

Riker's Island or "The Island," as it was popularly known was never a fun place to be, not as a prisoner anyhow. After the judge denied bail, KD was hauled off to The Island among a bus full of prisoners. Upon arrival, they were split up into groups and placed in bullpens. Slowly, the guards initiated their intake process. They were thoroughly searched. Their street clothes were replaced with inmate greens. For dinner, they were served spaghetti and meatballs as they went through the intake process.

After the intake process, they were ushered into another bullpen where they awaited the guards to escort them to their respective housing units. KD now wore a green jumpsuit, transforming from the King that he was to an inmate. The reality was slowly setting in. His injuries had yet to heal fully, but according to the state, he was a stone-cold killer.

How does one go from defending himself in a robbery to becoming a prisoner? No doubt, KD was treated unfairly in the situation. Had they given him bail or bond, then he'd have been able to heal and receive the necessary medical attention that he desperately needed. Being in the state custody where they provided the bare minimum, KD would be lucky if he received the prescribed medications.

There was also the danger of not knowing who was who. KD was in an environment where gang activities and violence were glorified. He needed eyes in the front, back and sides at all times. The last thing he wanted was to be mixed up in someone else's beef. Bad enough he was not fully healed, which meant he was at a disadvantage. He couldn't wait to get to his housing unit so he'd be able to call home. He needed his uncle and he needed him now.

After about three hours of waiting, they were finally escorted to their housing units. Once KD settled in and received his pin code, he got in line to use the phone. He waited patiently for his turn and called his uncle. He couldn't get through so he tried Ms. Gladys. He was lucky this time. She answered the phone and she just so happened to be with Black. KD spoke with Black briefly, during which Black assured him he'd take care of him. KD ended the call in good spirits.

KD received a visit from Ms. Gladys the next day. He was happy to see her and was even happier to discover that she brought him white t-shirts, boxers, and money. Ms. Gladys urged KD to stay patient and assured him that Black had a team of lawyers working on his case. That was probably the best news he'd heard since he left the club with Dolla that night. It was a matter of waiting. KD felt like he didn't belong there but fighting a system designed to victimize you, he'd just have to prove his case in court.

On Riker's, days turned into weeks and weeks into months. KD received frequent attorney visits as well as visits from Ms. Gladys and occasionally, Black. Karen had even been down to see him once. He had more money than needed on his commissary. During his fifth month, he was granted a bail hearing. His team of attorneys did their job and his bail was set at an outrageous quarter million dollars. The judge ordered him to wear a monitoring device on his ankle, placing him on house arrest.

This was no money to Black, especially when it came to the freedom of his nephew. Within hours of returning from court, a bondsman was present with KD's bond in hand, ready to free him. Present with the bondsman were Black himself and two of his attorneys. Black was determined to free his nephew at all costs, and he was going to do it that same day.

In a matter of about three hours, KD was a free man. He'd adhere to the senseless conditions of his release because to him, freedom was the most important.

Chapter 26: NINE

Ten years in a maximum state penitentiary didn't teach Nine much. He was more ruthless now, with an even bigger chip on his shoulder than before he went away. Fortunately for him, his life sentence had been terminated by the Court of Appeals. The court, in its reversal decision, held that Nine was mentally unstable at the time of the crime, ordering him released from custody immediately to undergo mental health treatment.

The battles that led to this decision hadn't been easy, of course. It took a third lawyer, whom Dre retained on Nine's behalf prior to his untimely demise, to win Nine's appeal. As a free man, Nine had undergone months of inpatient mental health treatment until deemed stable enough for society. Although he was still subject to outpatient care, going from a dangerously filthy maximum prison cell to the streets of New York City was a trade-off that Nine very much appreciated.

It took Nine some time to readjust and transition

back to normal life. Through Tone, a long time and an only friend, Nine met his current girlfriend, Tiffany, with whom he shared an apartment. Tone hadn't stopped at introducing Nine to Tiffany. He went on to make Nine a partner in his highly lucrative weed operation, earning Nine thousands of dollars week after week.

With the help of Tone, things fell into place for Nine. But even with his freedom, a girlfriend that loved him dearly, a friend that treated him better than family, and the opportunity to earn a living, misery remained a friend of Nine's. The death of Dre, his only brother, while he served time in prison was one thing he couldn't bring himself to digest. It killed him day in and day out to wake up to the realization that his baby brother was killed because he wasn't there to protect him.

The guilt overwhelmed him daily, the reason he'd made it his duty to seek justice for his baby brother. Since becoming a free man, finding out who was responsible for Dre's murder had been a priority on his agenda. To him, avenging Dre's death was the closest thing to honoring his baby brother. And that was the reason he and Tone sat in Tone's hoopty in the darkness of the same back block Dre used to hustle on.

Through his sources, Nine discovered that the block had something to do with his brother's murder, and if that was the case, then he needed answers from whoever owned the block now. For months, Nine and Tone staked out the block and practically knew how the hustlers operated. Tonight was no different as they observed a young thug come into view on a pedal bike from around the corner. "Here we go." Nine said aloud, keeping a close eye on the thug as he rode slowly down the block.

Nine watched Biker Boy scan both sides of the street, oblivious to the fact that he was being watched. When Biker Boy reached in his pocket, Nine gripped his nine-millimeter tightly. He watched Biker Boy make a quick call on his cell, all the while riding slowly down to the end of the block. Having observed this on numerous occasions, Nine and Tone knew exactly what was taking place.

When Biker Boy stylishly made a U-turn at the corner and rode back in the opposite direction, Nine became excited. Night after night, they've watched a similar episode transpire. They watched Biker Boy make another call as he got to the middle of the block.

"This is gonna be easy," Nine said to Tone as he shifted in his seat.

In no time, two other thugs emerged from the same corner Biker Boy originated, one carrying a backpack on his back and the other with his hands in his hoodie pockets.

"I'm telling you, son on the right gotta be the muscle," Tone commented to Nine.

139

Nine continued to watch the two thugs with the duffle bag as they passed Biker Boy. He then said, "You're probably right, man. But I think son on the bike is strapped too."

"No doubt!" Tone shot back.

Nine and Tone watched on as the Backpack Boys ducked inside one of the buildings as they had done on many nights. Biker Boy slowly rode up and down the block on watch. When Nine and Tone saw Biker Boy reach for his phone a third time, they took it as their cue to move. Based on their previous observations, they knew more likely than not, the Backpack Boys were ready to exit the building.

Nine and Tone exited the hoopty and walked toward Biker Boy, who had his back to them. Biker Boy must've been about thirty feet from where the hoopty was parked but it hadn't taken Tone but a few seconds to cover the distance.

"Yo, my man, you got a light?" Tone asked as he approached Biker Boy.

Biker Boy quickly turned around, his face registering shock. He was caught so off guard that his initial reaction was to reach for his pistol, but Tone was a lot quicker on the draw.

"Don't even think about it, homie!" Tone barked, pointing his pistol at Biker Boy's chest.

Biker Boy froze at the sight of Tone's pistol. He hadn't heard Tone approaching and as he stared at the barrel of Tone's pistol, he knew it could be the end of him if he didn't play it right. Even if he made it out alive, he'd still have to explain to his boss why he was not on point.

"You got it, man. Just don't shoot!" Biker boy said in an attempt to diffuse the situation.

"Show me your hands!" Tone barked.

Biker Boy hesitantly raised both hands up off the bike's handlebars. Tone moved closer and removed a black pistol along with an iPhone from Biker Boy's pockets.

"Now let's play a little game," Tone said as he stuffed the pistol and phone in his own hoodie pocket. He then added, "When I say *go*, you'll ride your bike over to that wall."

Biker Boy nodded in agreement.

"Go!" Tone commanded and followed Biker Boy out of view and into the darkness.

$$$$$

Nine patiently lurked by the entrance of the building, the element of surprise clearly in his favor as he waited for the Backpack Boys to make their exit. Just as he expected, they came strolling out a moment later with their black backpack. Nine watched the two exit the building and made sure they were alone before emerging out of the shadows

141

with his pistol.

"Surprise, muthafuckas!" Nine barked, pointing his pistol at the thug in the hoodie.

The young thug carrying the backpack attempted to make a run for it. If he could re-enter the building, maybe he could prevent the stick-up. Unfortunately for him, though, the front door was locked.

"Dumb muthafucka!" Nine said as he shot the thug in the buttocks area.

"Aaaah!" The thug cried out in pain, still wearing the backpack on his back.

The thug in the hoodie attempted to use the distraction to draw his pistol but couldn't get it out of his pocket for some reason. That didn't stop him, though. He popped off a wild shot through his pocket, which grazed the left sleeve of Nine's black Champion sweater. Nine retaliated instantaneously, sending a shot into the young thug's right shoulder.

"Fuck!" The young thug cussed and toppled over in pain.

Nine quickly disarmed the young thug. Afterwards, he walked over to the thug with the ass wound and freed him of his backpack. Slinging it over his shoulder, Nine pointed a pistol each at the thugs on the pavement then said, "I'll let you dumb muthafuckas live, only because I need y'all to deliver a message for me," Nine paused before adding, "Tell your boss Nine was here!"

With that, Nine took off in the direction of Tone. As he passed Tone and Biker Boy, "We out, son," was all he said without stopping.

Tone turned to Biker Boy and said, "Get your boys to the emergency room." He then joined Nine in the direction of the hoopty. They jumped in the hoopty and got out of dodge with quickness. While Tone drove, Nine inspected the contents of the heavy backpack — nothing but dollar bills. Driving to one of Tone's spots, they changed clothes and replaced the hoopty with a Navigator. They then headed to a neighborhood bar for drinks. Not only did they send a message, but they also made a come up in the process. It was a win-win move.

Chapter 27: ATTENTION

Nine took one last pull and sent the cigarette butt flying out of the front passenger window of Tone's Caddy. As he exhaled the cigarette smoke, he asked Tone, "Yo, whatchu think these muthafuckas up to?"

"Fuck if I know," came Tone's harsh response from the driver's seat.

"Rolling in my Caddy with my bubble-butt shawty, plus she holds the shottie..." *Caddy Muzik*, a track by Joe Dawg, an underground dancehall artist, banged through the Caddy's speakers.

Nine shook his head in disapproval before saying, "I'm saying, though, it's been over a month. You mean to tell me them muthafuckas don't give a fuck about the money we took from them?"

"I don't know about them cowards but I know if anybody touched any of my hard-earned money, I'll move heaven and earth till I find their ass." Tone shot back with conviction.

"That means they're either gonna make a sneaky move or they're just gonna eat the loss. Either way, they will look soft." Nine said.

"Don't sleep on nobody in these streets, man. Because the moment you do, you become lunch meat." Tone cautioned.

Nine nodded in agreement before saying, "That's definitely true, fam. Matter of fact, what block is this, Morris?"

Tone nodded in response.

"Roll through Grant and let me see something," Nine instructed and Tone complied, making a left-hand turn.

At the next intersection, "Whatchu got in mind, man?" Tone inquired as he made a right-hand turn onto Grant. He knew Nine was a hot-head so he wanted to be prepared.

There was no response from Nine but Tone knew what time it was when he saw Nine draw his pistol.

"Slow down," Nine instructed, rolling the front passenger window all the way down.

Tone eased the Caddy down to a creep as he looked from one side of the street to the next. A small crowd hung on either side of the block. Without warning, Nine stuck the pistol out of the window and squeezed. Shot after shot without a specific target, Nine squeezed off about four shots before the fifth round jammed on him. A few shots came from the gathered crowd but Tone was already on the move.

"Let's go, let's go!" Nine barked, ducking in his seat.

Tone already had the pedal to the floor in the direction of Sherman Street. With the speed and skill of a Nascar driver, Tone maneuvered the Caddy out of the area.

"That should get their attention," Nine finally said as Tone made a left-hand turn onto Webster Avenue.

"Yo you're a dumb muthafucka, you know that?" Tone asked but Nine was in no mood to converse.

Chapter 28: LEAN ON' EM

The Hill-Top Inn motel, even with its freshly manicured lawns and new paint job, was none other than your average hole-in-the-wall. Aside from the basics — bed, bath, basic cable, refrigerator, and microwave — the place had nothing else to offer. But for seventy bucks a night, it served as a safe haven for Nine. The recent shooting of his baby mama's house, among other things, has prompted him to put some distance between himself and the people he loved.

With a bag of Chinese take-out in his left hand, Nine approached and unlocked the door to his room. No sooner than Nine entered and shut the door behind him that his cellphone rang. Setting the bag of food onto the nightstand, he unclipped his phone off his hip and studied the screen for a moment.

"Fuck?" He wondered, tossing the phone onto the bed in frustration.

The alarm clock on the nightstand read 6:17 p.m.

Nine rushed off to the bathroom to relieve himself. The dull smell in the bathroom made Nine wish he had some air freshener. No worries, he'll just have to pick one up later. After using the bathroom, he returned to the bedroom where he placed his nine-millimeter handgun on the nightstand. Seating himself on the bed, he rolled a spliff and lit it. With the black remote control, he switched on the small television and began surfing through channels. Finding nothing interesting, he settled on Music Choice's hip-hop channel. The sound of Young Money's *Bedrock* filled the room almost instantly.

He puffed away on his spliff until he was satisfied, and then placed it in the ashtray on the nightstand. It was time to attack the beef and broccoli platter he carried inside with him. Bite after bite, Nine devoured the entire platter, taking sips of a Diet Coke along the way. After eating, Nine decided to sit back and let his food digest. He glanced at the clock, 6:58 p.m. He grabbed his phone to call Toya, his sidepiece. Before he could dial her number, though, his phone rang. It was the same unfamiliar number that called him earlier.

"Fuck could this be?" He wondered. He waited for the phone to stop ringing. The voicemail icon soon appeared on the phone's screen. Nine quickly dialed one to listen to the voicemail, anxious to know who the caller was. As he listened to the message, a disgusted look appeared on his face. Nine pressed one to repeat the message a first, then a second time.

"Call!" A male voice said with authority.

Erasing the message, Nine ended the call, making a mental note to find out who had the audacity to disrespect his phone like that. He dialed Toya's number and listened as it rang. No answer. He quickly hung up and tried again.

"Hello!" Toya answered with an attitude.

He heard a piercing scream from a child in the background. "Damn, did I do something wrong, T?" Nine countered coyly.

"I'm sorry, boo. Stinky over here screaming his head off like somebody is killing him, got me aggravated," Toya apologized and explained.

"What's wrong with him?" Nine asked.

"Nothing, he is just acting up," Toya responded.

"Oh. Anyway, am I gonna see you tonight?" Nine pressed.

"Well, I'm waiting for my babysitter to get here. Why don't you text me the address to where you're at and I'll call you when I'm ready," Toya shot back.

"Okay, baby. I'll text it to you in a minute," Nine said before hanging up the phone. He wasted no time texting the address of the motel to Toya along with directions. He fired up the other half of his spliff and puffed away. As he smoked, he picked up his cell and dialed the unfamiliar number. He'd been itching to know to whom that voice belonged. Nine held the phone to his ear and listened as the phone just rang and rang. Frustrated, he was about to hang up when someone finally picked up the other end. Strangely, no voice was heard, just background music.

"Yo!" Nine barked into the phone, still no answer. By now, the steam rose out of Nine's ears. He cursed himself for even calling the unfamiliar number back in the first place.

"Yo!" Nine growled into the phone angrily.

"Now that I got your attention," a calm voice began from the other end, "I'mma keep this very brief." The voice added then paused.

It was the same voice that left the voicemail. "Man, who the fuck is this?!" Nine barked into the phone, trying to use the pause to his advantage.

No sooner than those words parted with his lips, the voice was back on the line, saying, "There's no need for none of that. As I was saying, I'm sure you know by now that you are not untouchable. What happened wasn't meant to hurt or scare you, but to show you that you can be touched in more ways than you can think of." There was another pause.

This time, Nine remained silent. He knew by now to whom the mystery voice belonged — the man responsible for the recent shooting of his baby-mama's house. A man he only knew as Black.

"As you can see," the voice began again, "We both have something to lose here, but the question is who'll lose the most. I'm a businessman and bloodshed is bad for business. Here is my offer: a chance to truce this whole thing up before it goes any further. Call me within the next week to set up a time and place to meet. If I don't hear from you, I'd take it you've decided otherwise."

With that, the line went dead before Nine even had a chance to get a word in. Nine fumed. *Who the fuck did Black think he was, giving him an ultimatum?* Nine thought about calling back just to ask that question but quickly decided against it. Instead, he decided to swallow his pride and make a compromise for the sake of his daughter. He'd play Black's game, but not for long!

Nine puffed his spliff to calm his raging nerves. He then called Toya to make sure she was still coming over. He definitely needed some stress relieving after that conversation.

Chapter 29: BLOWING MONEY

It was a sunny spring Friday. KD and Poundz had plans to hit up Fordham Road and pick up a few things. Maybe they would cap the day off with a trip to Jay-z's 40-40 Club in Manhattan. At some time after one in the afternoon, KD drove his Range Rover to Poundz's place. He parked up front and called Poundz, who emerged from the front door moments later.

"This baby can use a bath, homie." Poundz commented as he got in the passenger seat and gave KD dap.

Taking heed to his man's comment, KD drove straight to Fordham Hand Jobs for a quick wash and detail combo. While the Range went through the wash, the two treated themselves to a spliff in front of the car wash. KD's cell phone buzzed, Black's number appearing on the screen.

"What's up, Unk?" KD answered.

"How you been, nephew?" Black asked before adding, "I hope you've been staying outta trouble."

"You know I am, Unk."

"Good for you, nephew," Black began and added, "Listen, we have some things to discuss so meet me at the club later."

"How late are we talking?" KD asked.

"Come have some drinks, I'm sure there'll be some broads there tonight. Oh, make sure to come by yourself," Black instructed, his way of telling KD to be there before the club closed.

KD assured Black he'd be there before hanging up. Ten minutes later, the Range emerged looking a lot cleaner than it had been a while ago. The Armor-all on the tires gave it an extra touch of class, garnering some attention to KD's ride. They jumped in the ride and pulled into traffic, impatient city drivers tooting their horns after them for cutting into traffic.

Hitting stores like Foot Locker, Doctor Jays and Sammy's Fashion, among others, they purchased a variety of clothing and accessories, ranging from sweat suits to jeans, footwear to fitted caps. At The Platinum Jewelry store on the corner of Fordham and the Grand Concourse, their last stop, KD picked up a pair of diamond earrings for himself and a matching his and hers diamond bracelets for Black and his mom.

Poundz purchased a chunky pinky ring. In a matter of about three hours, the two spent nearly ten thousand dollars. They were sure the storeowners appreciated their visits.

From the jewelry store, they drove to KD's apartment, picking up some Caribbean food on the way. At KD's apartment, they smoked two spliffs, ate their food, and smoked more spliffs. The two drove to Grant Ave around eight o'clock to check in with Cash. The block was all business as usual.

"Take me by Morris so I can pick up this bread," Poundz said as they left Grant.

After the quick pick up, KD dropped Poundz and his bags off at his place. Of course, he had to help him carry them upstairs just like he had done for him. Poundz was disappointed when he learned that they couldn't hang out due to KD's sudden meeting with Black.

"Is all good, I'll call up Renee to keep me company," Poundz said while they stood together in his apartment.

"There you go, always keep one in the cut for nights like this," said KD in response.

"Holla at me in the a.m. and let me know what's up," said Poundz as they exchanged daps.

"You already, baby," said KD as he walked out.

Chapter 30: THE TRUCE

It was after ten when KD returned to his apartment. Taking a hot shower, he treated himself to a double-shot of Hennessy and a fat spliff. He threw on a light hoodie and a dab of Izzy Miyaki, tucked his .45 in his waist, grabbed his phone and car keys, and headed out the door. Jay-Z's *The Blueprint* kept him company on the ride down to the club. It was about twenty past midnight when he walked through the club's backdoor.

Black was happy to see KD as usual. They exchanged a manly hug before he led KD into his office, where Danja awaited. Once seated and their glasses filled, Black lit a spliff he just rolled and said with a trace of concern in his voice, "I'm glad I can count on you, nephew."

"Is everything alright, Unk?" KD asked, expressing his concern for his uncle.

Black puffed away on the spliff before responding. "Life couldn't be better," he said then added, "We finally got an opportunity to fix our little situation tonight."

KD remained silent, just sipping his Hennessy.

"Our friend Nine has agreed to meet tonight so we can reach an understanding." Black said, passing the spliff to KD.

KD nodded attentively.

Black continued, "Now, I want you to talk to him face to face, man to man and sort this thing out once and for all." He knocked on his office desk to emphasize his point.

KD nodded again, beginning to understand the situation.

Danja remained silent, giving an occasional nod as the two conversed.

"Convince him to bury this problem permanently," Black spoke again before adding, "Make him an offer that he can't refuse and once he accepts, extend him the opportunity for a business relationship."

"You're right, Unk," KD finally spoke, "This situation is bad for business and needs to be addressed immediately!" He added, passing the spliff back to Black.

Black didn't speak right away so KD used that as an opportunity to continue. Out of curiosity, he asked, "But tell me something, Unk. How and when did you get Nine to succumb to this meeting, and who selected the time and venue?"

"He called me a few days ago and agreed to meet. Of course I influenced his decision. For the second part of your question, he selected the time and place to meet," Black said coolly before adding, "Expect him here around three."

"Good, we can finally bury this problem and move on," said KD.

"You can handle this, right, nephew?" Black asked with a smirk.

"Of course, Unk," KD shot back before adding, "Besides, I'm the one who pulled the trigger."

Black's expression was suddenly serious again. He said, "This is your meeting. I'll be here, but only to ensure that it goes well. I'll have a few of my guys stay back. Now go have some fun, but remember... around three o'clock." With that, Black started shuffling paperwork on his desk, his way of dismissing KD. KD had a lot of love for his uncle and Black loved him like a son, so he didn't let little things like these irritate his pride. After all, Black is the reason why he is in the position that he is in today.

KD walked out to the club area and had a seat at the bar. Stacy, the redheaded bartender spotted him and quickly brought him a double-shot of Hennessy. She returned to serving her customers, chatting KD up whenever she got a break.

KD was in a world of his own, his mindset on his

meeting. Here he was, getting ready to face a man whose only brother he'd murdered years ago. He'd have to look Nine in his eyes and tell him to bury their beef forever.

Would Nine be able to compose himself? And if he doesn't, should KD blow his brains out like he had done his brother? What would be a good icebreaker? KD pondered as he sat at the bar nursing his glass of Hennessy.

He heard the DJ announce *last call for alcohol*, and that was when he finally checked the time. It was a half past three.

The crowd started to thin out sometime after that. The bouncers began ushering the drunks to their rides. At a quarter till four, the DJ announced that the club was closed and patrons began to spill out into the parking lot. By four, the parking lot was nearly cleared.

Still no sign of Nine.

KD retreated to Black's office where he helped him and Danja sort out and count the night's cash.

Four-fifteen, still no sign of Nine.

KD became concerned and it showed on his face. Was this fool toying with them? They'll find out sooner than later.

Four-thirty, still no Nine.

The three men continued to put the bills together in the right denominations. They each clutched a spliff between their lips while they worked.

The more KD tried to remain hopeful, the more the situation looked like a bust. Yet, he wouldn't dare give up on his uncle.

Suddenly, the men heard a loud crashing sound. Then boom, an explosion from the club area. All three men instinctively hit the floor. The furniture around them vibrated violently. They heard the screams, and a series of thunderous booms that followed.

"This way!" Danja bellowed over the loudness that surrounded them.

KD and Black followed.

Explosion after explosion, KD counted five before he lost count because they were on the move. Machine guns were ablaze as the building went up in flames.

"What the fuck? Sounds like a war zone!" KD said as he followed Black and Danja down a dark tunnel-like exit.

Danja used his cell phone to provide a ray of lighting for what felt like eternity in that cobwebbed tunnel. Finally, they came up on a dusty door. Danja must've used all his might to break the door open. Before KD realized, they stood on the pavement outside disoriented.

"This way!" Danja said and the three took off running down the block like mad men.

They ran down and across the street, then around the corner. They ran so fast that although KD lost count, he was almost sure it was over ten blocks. The sirens of ambulances and fire trucks pierced their eardrums as they ran by them. All KD could think was *Nine, the slimy bastard!*

From a couple of blocks away, they hailed a cab to a bodega around the corner from KD's apartment and walked the rest of the way.

Once they were in the apartment, KD gathered a few things, including the contents of his safes while Black and Danja tried to make sense of what just transpired. When KD finished packing, the men hauled ass to Jersey in KD's BMW.

Every news channel seemed to show a rerun of the remains of Blackstar, the once popular nightclub and hangout. While Black and Danja discretely returned to New York to sort out the mess, KD was forced to remain in Jersey. In Black's house in Jersey, his days turned into weeks, then months, ultimately becoming a permanent residence for him.

Chapter 31: DOLLA

The incident at Blackstar made headlines across America. News outlets around the country, from radio to television to newspapers all told their version of the story. While some dubbed it a terrorist attack, others, a simple act of violence. As the media always did, they speculated as to the motive behind the incident. It became the topic of discussion on social media sites.

Dolla was in the kitchen of Angel's house, smoking a spliff and making breakfast when he heard an anchorman from the morning news reporting about the incident. Upon hearing *Blackstar*, he hurried to the living room where he caught a video clip of the nightclub ablaze. It was a short clip but enough to show the sign and the bullet-riddled front door of the club with its broken windows.

"Get the fuck outta here!" Dolla said aloud as he grabbed the remote to turn up the volume.

"A dozen bodies have been recovered from what was left of the nightclub, six of whom have been identified.

It appears that this six include the club's owner, his young son, an associate and three employees. Six bodies remain unidentified. The NYPD is asking for anybody with information..."

Dolla was on the phone before the anchorman could finish his sentence. He dialed KD's number, no answer. He tried his brother, no answer. Black's cell, still no answer. Dolla was dying inside. He hoped that this was all a mistake. His frustration grew by the second. He tried Karen's cell and got some luck.

"Hello," Karen answered.

"You've been watching the news, ma?" Dolla asked.

"Well, good morning to you too. I haven't even had my coffee yet. Why, what happened?" Karen shot back.

Dolla's phone beeped, it was Poundz. "Make me a cup. I'm on my way!" Dolla simply said before clicking over. "Yo!" He then barked into the phone.

"What's good, fam?" Poundz asked in response.

"Yo, what the fuck is that shit on the news about?" Dolla asked impatiently. He was desperate for answers.

"I heard about it this morning. I ain't believe it so I drove to the spot myself, this shit is real, fam. New York's finest is still on the scene." Pound's answered.

"When was the last time you spoke to K or Black?" Asked Dolla.

"I was with K most of yesterday. We even had plans to hit the 40/40 but he left my crib around ten, saying he had to go meet Black at the club. I ain't heard from neither of them since," answered Poundz.

"You tried calling?"

"Homie, I've been calling K since I heard about that shit, no answer. I tried Black a few times too, same shit. I'm driving to K's crib as we speak."

"Hit me when you get there, man." Dolla told his brother then hung up. He had been moving so fast that he hadn't even realized that he'd been sitting in Karen's parking lot. He got out of the car and walked to the door. Karen opened the door with a steaming cup of coffee in hand.

"Just as you ordered, sir," She said jokingly, still unaware of what was going on.

Dolla took the cup and followed Karen inside her living room. The television was tuned to a news channel with a meteorologist giving a seven-day forecast but none of that mattered to Dolla. He needed to know what was going on and he needed it soon.

"I've been watching the news since you called and I haven't seen nothing interesting so what's all the hype about?" Karen finally asked.

"Twist something up, ma! Some crazy shit has happened down bottom and I need to figure out what the fuck is going on," Dolla responded.

163

Dolla lit a Newport and sipped his hot coffee in silence. The stress was evident on his face. His cell buzzed, Poundz again. "Talk to me, b," answered Dolla quickly.

"Yo, I don't understand this shit, son." Poundz shot back.

"What happened, b, talk to me," Dolla pressed on.

"Ain't nobody here and what I'm looking at doesn't make any sense," Poundz responded.

Karen lit the spliff and passed it to Dolla, who snatched it and took a long pull.

"A few things are missing out of the bedroom and the big closet. Safes are empty and the keys to his range and the Beamer Black just bought him are both gone." Dolla said.

"Safes are empty and two car keys missing? What the fuck?" Dolla shot back.

"Well, he was in the Range when he left my crib last night and I know for sure he ain't driving two cars," Poundz responded.

"This shit doesn't make any sense but I don't wanna jump to conclusions. Have you tried his mom's?" Dolla said, passing the spliff back to Karen.

"No answer, she might be at work but I'mma stop by her crib."

"Son, did K tell you why he was meeting with

164

Black?"

"Nah. Just that Black wanted to speak to him about something."

"Find out as much as you can and keep me posted. And have Ms. Gladys call me whenever you speak to her."

"Gotchu, fam, one love!"

"One!" Dolla said before hanging up.

Karen looked at Dolla as if to say *what's happened?* She had been surfing through channels on the television and on social media while Dolla was on the phone.

"Here and do you mind telling me what's going on, Dolla?" The question came just as Dolla expected.

Dolla took the spliff and said, "I don't know yet, ba-by-girl. All I know is what's on the news. My brother doesn't know much, said he just found out this morning but I promise I'll let you know as soon as I find out. We're all in this together."

Dolla rolled another spliff for the two to share before leaving to tend to some business.

Chapter 32: SACRIFICE

A week went by and Dolla still hadn't made much progress regarding the Blackstar incident. Poundz's push for information came to a standstill. He'd even gone as far as offering a reward for information but his efforts had been to no avail. KD's mom had been very devastated, with not much to say. Karen's daily phone calls to her brother hadn't yielded much information. So far, Dolla had nothing to work with, regarding who is responsible for the incident.

Police investigations were still *ongoing*. As if that wasn't bad enough, Poundz told him that the bodies of Black and KD had been identified, released, and will soon be cremated. Their funerals will definitely be a must-attend event. As Dolla contemplated his options, he faced numerous unanswered questions. Was it truly a terrorist attack? Was it an act from an enemy of Black's or KD's, or maybe both? Were Black and his workers simply collateral damage? All this and Poundz didn't have a clue as to who the culprit was.

Dolla had to make a tough decision and soon. He could remain on the run and watch their whole empire crumble or he could say fuck it and take his chances. *What would KD do?* Dolla wondered as he pondered on the issue. Option two meant returning to the city, finding out who was responsible for the attack, and handling it how he saw fit, while avoiding capture by the police.

At this point, he had enough money stashed to just say fuck it, cut his losses, and move to the Caribbean or South America or even Africa and start all over. But doing that would be very selfish of him. How about his family and their legacy? How about the bond they developed over the years? How about what he believed in? The respect, the love, and the loyalty for his brothers? From the start, they had been selfless when it came to the family and nothing was big enough to change that, not even this incident.

As Dolla sat in Angel's living room, easing his stress with a fat spliff, and reminiscing about the old days, he told himself that his family's legacy MUST live on. He used the next few days to tighten up any loose ends and select his replacement for the time he'd be gone. This was a mystery trip that he may or may not return from.

Dolla gave Gutter, his next in command more room and freedom to run the crew. He made sure the Brownville crew had at least a six-month supply of product before handing things over fully to Gutter. He spent some time with Karen, comforting her and promising to handle the situation regardless of the costs.

Finally, Dolla hit the road on a quiet and cool night. Riding in the car with him were two duffle bags, one filled with clothes and the other cash, and his trusty Desert Eagle. He drove most of the way in silence, contemplating a plan of action upon arrival. Taking the Tappan Zee Bridge, Dolla entered the city by way of Yonkers and made a safe and easy arrival to his final destination.

Chapter 33: CHESS PIECES

Dolla awoke from a good night's sleep around eight the next morning, feeling a bit at ease. He treated himself to a fat spliff before his morning shower. He left the hotel around nine-thirty in search of a decent place for breakfast. Luckily, he didn't have to drive far; he found a mom-n-pop diner about a mile from the hotel. He enjoyed a cup of hot chocolate and browsed the Daily News as he awaited his meal. When it arrived, he picked at it, contemplating his plan of action.

Midway through his meal, he decided to contact Poundz, who agreed to meet him for lunch at a familiar Caribbean cuisine restaurant. After he hung up with Poundz, the food no longer appealed to him so he paid the bill and left the diner.

Awake and somewhat fed, he was ready to take on the day's mission. On the drive back to the hotel, he found himself fantasizing about the sweet taste of revenge, the pain and destruction he planned to bring into the life of the culprit responsible for the incident.

As far as he knew, the NYPD's investigation was at a standstill, and that was reason enough to even the score without feeling an iota of guilt on his conscience. Finding the culprit wouldn't be an easy task, but Dolla was determined to find out. So engrossed in his daydreaming, he hadn't even realized that he had been sitting in the hotel parking lot for fifteen minutes with the engine running.

He finally shut the car off and went upstairs to his room, constantly reminding himself that revenge would soon be his. Upstairs, he lay down to relax before his meeting with Poundz but he was quickly absorbed by his thoughts. He was still a wanted man, whom if caught, could face a life sentence. He could not afford to ignore the fact that they were involved in a dirty game. In the situation he found himself in, only true warriors survived. It was time for decisions, hard decisions. Treating the situation like a game of chess was a must. That meant leaving no stones unturned and striking at precise moments.

At 1:30 p.m., he drove to the restaurant where he was supposed to meet Poundz. He arrived at about two-fifteen and noticed that Poundz was already seated at a table in the back of the restaurant. As he walked through the place to join his baby brother, he took some time to acknowledge the few familiar faces that he recognized. The sweet sounds of reggae music filled the air inside the restaurant.

Poundz stood as Dolla approached and the two embraced in a long manly hug. "Good to see you, brother," said Dolla as they separated.

"Good to see you too." Poundz responded, returning to his seat.

A tray carrying a pitcher of iced tea and two empty glasses graced the center of their table, proving this restaurant's home-like atmosphere. Dolla seated himself across from his brother and gave him one good look-over. Poundz didn't appear too worked up under all the stress he'd been faced with lately. Actually, he appeared normal, and that was exactly how Dolla wanted him. They were about to have a very important conversation, and Dolla needed him focused just as he was.

A young waitress brought them some cocoa bread and took their meal orders — steamed red snapper with white rice for Dolla and curry goat with white rice for Poundz.

"So what's been going on?" Dolla asked after the waitress walked away.

"I've been trying to figure that out myself, man," Poundz responded, shaking his head.

"You ain't heard anything new?" Dolla pressed on.

"I just found out that two of the bodies were Nine's people," Poundz said before adding, "Who is Nine? Dre's older brother who just came home after spanking a body.

171

All that tells me is that this whole thing could be over Dre's death." Poundz continued to update Dolla with the bit of information he managed to gather through his sources. Information regarding Nine's whereabouts was very limited at that point.

The waitress brought their meals and they dug into them right away. Over the course of their meal, Dolla laid out the game plan they would adapt from that point forward. Dolla declared war on Nine and anybody around him. Evening the score was Dolla's main concern. They had enough manpower and machinery, not to mention the funds to go to war for as long as it may take. That was precisely the route that Dolla planned to go.

First, they must rally up their troops. Dolla asked for a mandatory meeting the next morning, requiring the presence of every soldier who played a part in their city operation. It didn't matter if they were just a lookout, he wanted everyone present. Dolla intended to show a very strong presence in the streets to let cats know they meant business. They were at war, a very deadly one indeed and there were going to be repercussions for anyone who got in their way.

When they finished their meals, Poundz called the young waitress over and whispered something in her ear. She nodded and disappeared to the kitchen. She returned a moment later with their check and a Styrofoam plate in a carry out bag. Poundz paid the check, leaving a healthy tip for the waitress. To the naked eye, everything seemed normal but Poundz and Dolla knew the contents of the Styrofoam plate in the carry out bag.

To say the least, they left the restaurant with a very solid game plan in place. Dolla followed Poundz back to his apartment, where they smoked some spliffs out of the haze given to them in the Styrofoam plate. They took some time, catching up on what was going on in their individual lives. Before Dolla left, Poundz offered him half of what was left of the fire haze and he gladly accepted. It was dark by the time he finally left his brother's apartment. He took the drive back to the hotel in a much better mood than when he woke up that morning.

Chapter 34: RALLY THE TROOPS

Upon arising the next morning, Dolla prepared himself mentally for his meeting with the soldiers. Considering all the factors, the weight laid on their shoulders to even the score. He took a long shower and got dressed. He smoked himself a nice spliff before heading to the hotel's lobby for breakfast. Over pancakes and turkey bacon, he thought hard about the situation they faced. Being that he was still a wanted man, the situation at hand placed him between a rock and a hard place.

After breakfast, he went back up to his room and smoked another spliff. He then drove to Poundz's apartment.

Poundz came to the door in a robe. The heavy stench of haze smacked Dolla dead in the face as he followed Poundz inside his apartment. In the living room, the big screen was tuned to ESPN. "Take a load off, man." Poundz said casually, seating himself in the recliner.

Dolla seated himself on the sofa across from

Poundz, who had a smirk on his face.

Poundz lit a freshly rolled spliff, took a long pull then said, "Dig this; I finally got some info on Nine."

That explains the smirk on his face. Dolla thought. "Solid?" Dolla asked.

"As can be for now," responded Poundz, taking another pull on the spliff before passing it to Dolla.

Dolla snatched the spliff and took a pull, thinking to himself that Poundz was right. They had so little information to work with that every little lead they could get had to be treated as a solid one.

"That's good; we can follow up on that and see how it turns out," Dolla said.

"We'll definitely have to 'cause this is supposed to be his baby mama's crib," Poundz said in agreement.

"How you come up on that?" Dolla asked.

In response, Poundz said, "Long story. My home-girl overheard his baby mama fighting with some bitch over him."

Dolla puffed away on the spliff, nodding his head at the progress they were making. He passed the spliff to Poundz, who walked off towards his bedroom with it. When Poundz returned moments later, fully dressed and ready to go, Dolla felt confident about his position. He was prepared to do anything to even things up with Nine. The two finished the spliff before leaving Poundz's apartment.

They decided to take Poundz's Expedition on the drive to the warehouse where the meeting with the soldiers was to take place. The abandoned warehouse was one of the properties they had purchased but never put to good use. Poundz called Cash, who was present at the warehouse with the soldiers. Upon arrival, they parked in the warehouse parking lot and headed inside where the soldiers awaited.

It appeared everybody was present and ready for the meeting. Dolla looked around the room and thought their crew had grown in numbers since the last time he was with them. He was impressed with the numbers and the faces that greeted them. Looking across the sea of hungry faces, he felt confident about the challenges they faced. Though, he'd intended to let Poundz handle the formalities, he decided against it. Getting his message across to the soldiers was his main concern. After dapping up Cash and a few others, Dolla decided to get the meeting underway.

"What's up, everybody?" Dolla began before adding, "Some of y'all know who I am and for those who don't, the name is Dolla. This here is my brother Poundz."

A few nods came from the sea of faces, a sure sign of respect.

"The reason I called y'all here this morning is to discuss a very important issue that we all face as a team,"

Dolla said then paused again to let it sink in.

"We're all aware of the tragic incident that took place a few months back, at the Blackstar night spot," Dolla paused again before adding, "For those who don't know, that incident claimed the lives of two key members of our family."

That stirred up murmurs among the soldiers.

"The time has come for us to even the score. From this point forward, we're at war!" Dolla's last statement drew serious faces around the room. That was the reaction he expected, and he truly appreciated it.

"Look at the man sitting next to you and tell him you got his back. If you had problems before, now is the time to bury your differences," Dolla said before adding, "There will be some bloodshed, you all should be willing to die for the man next to you."

No one said a word, just serious faces around the room. Dolla knew then that he'd gotten his message across. He spoke for a few more minutes before opening the floor up for questions. Before ending the meeting, he assured them that they would pass any necessary information down the channel.

Chapter 35: CASUALTIES OF WAR

If there was any such thing as bad luck in this life, then Nine would be the epitome of such. From the beginning, Nine's life had been doomed, and the past two weeks had just been hell for him. "Why me?" Was the question he'd been asking himself repeatedly. As if losing both parents at such a young age wasn't enough, he'd endured ten years of maximum state penitentiary time. Then he'd lost Dre, the only other family he had left.

Now, here was his daughter's mother, lying in a hospital bed wrapped up in bandages with ninety-five percent of her body burned up. To make a bad situation worse, the same incident that landed Tiffany in a hospital bed caused the state of New York to take temporary custody of Sasha, his only child. The thought of Tiffany lying helpless and hopeless in her hospital bed alone brought Nine to tears.

Nine was slowly turning into an uncontrollable animal and who could blame him? Having your only child abducted and your child's mother's house burned down while she was tied up inside was reason enough.

"I'll finish this! They started this shit but I will finish it!" Nine said to Tone, who was twisting a spliff for the two to share.

"Word! We're gonna handle these muthafuckas!" Tone said as he continued to put the finishing touches on the spliff.

The E&J bottle they had been drinking from was nearly empty.

"I want them muthafuckas to feel pain!" Nine said, slamming his fist into the coffee table for emphasis. The force from his fist sent two remote controls and a cigarette pack crashing to the carpet.

"No question! Those evil bastards need to pay for this shit," Tone responded, puffing away on the spliff he just twisted.

Nine took a swig from the E&J bottle and added, "They wanna fuck with me, I'll show them the real meaning of evil."

"I got Tre and them ready to go, all you gotta do is say when," Tone said, passing the spliff to Nine.

Nine took a long pull then said, "This shit is personal, son." He then added, "I wanna touch them myself. I wanna look them in their eyes when I bring pain to'em!"

179

"I feel you, homie," Tone took a sip of the liquor and nodded in agreement.

He warned Nine against avenging Dre's supposed killer from the beginning but Nine disregarded his advice. Now they both found themselves knee-deep in drama. Like he'd been doing since Nine came home from prison, though, Tone continued to ride with his man. All the two had was each other, and Tone knew one-hundred percent that Nine would do the same for him.

"Yo, you know I got your back no matter what. I just wish you would've listened to me in the beginning," Tone said calmly.

Nine took one last pull then passed the spliff back to Tone. He then said, "It's too late for all that finger-pointing now, man. I'm riding tonight, you with me or not?"

That statement rubbed Tone the wrong way. He'd been nothing but a friend to Nine from the start. In response, Tone said, "Don't even play yourself, homie! You know I gotchu." A hint of anger marked Tone's voice.

"I mean no harm; this shit just got me fucked up, homie." Nine said before sticking out his right fist and adding, "Hit up Tre and them and let's do this!"

Tone bumped fists with Nine before removing his phone from his hip and making a call. As he did that, Nine ducked into the hallway and returned with a green military-style duffle bag. He unzipped the bag to reveal an assortment of guns and boxes of ammunition. Nine inspected the guns and ammunition.

Nine was ready to ride and it showed.

Chapter 36: WARTIME

It had been one hell of a month. The war between their family and Nine was in full throttle. Although they had yet to have any luck as far as Nine's whereabouts, they managed to land a few key blows, powerful enough to tip Nine over the edge. Robbing a few of his weed houses for several pounds and a couple of thousand dollars in cash was the initial blow. The icing on the cake was the message they sent Nine through one of his workers.

The recent home invasion which resulted in the kidnapping of Nine's daughter and the torching of his baby mama's house with her tied up inside was the most powerful thus far. In their desperate search for Nine, they planted these seeds in hopes to bring Nine out of hiding.

"Yo, I'm taking Face and Bam with me back to Westchester," Dolla said to Poundz as he passed him the spliff.

"I'mma lay low in the hood and keep my ears open," Poundz shot back in response.

They were inside Manny's garage, one of the many businesses they had acquired over the years. While it generated lots of clean money through regular business, it afforded them lots of other benefits. Not only did they use it to customize their rides, but its location provided for a perfect meeting space. Since the beginning of the war with Nine, they made it a headquarters and staging area for planning and carrying out their attacks.

"Please keep some shooters with you, and definitely keep your eyes and ears open," Dolla pleaded with his brother. The last thing he wanted was to lose another person close to him.

"I gotchu, big brother," responded Poundz.

"Let's see what that fool does in the next few days." With that, the two exchanged daps and a long hug.

Dolla got in the backseat of his purring Escalade, where Face and Bam, Dolla's most trusted shooters awaited in the driver and passenger seats, respectively. A moment later, the garage door retracted upwards and into the streets they went, followed by Poundz and his entourage. The two headed in opposite directions. About thirty minutes later, Face eased the Escalade into the driveway of Dolla's secluded safe house. Dolla purchased the three-bedroom house through Donna, a realtor he had dated on and off some time back. While it wasn't much, it served the purpose of a safe haven in a time like this.

Face inched the truck forward in the driveway until

the overhead door to the garage retracted upwards. Once the door was fully upward, Face pulled the truck inside the garage and cut off the ignition. The three men exited the vehicle as they watched the door retract down. While Face made sure the garage door was secured, Dolla unlocked the door to the main house and Bam led them inside, gun in hand like he'd been doing routinely night in and out.

As Dolla fingered the house's alarm panel, Face and Bam checked the entire house for threats. The two joined Dolla in the living room, assuring him that the house was clear of threats. Wasting no time, Dolla gave the two their usual instructions before he stormed off into his bedroom. He rolled himself a fat spliff and lit it. As he smoked, he decided to take a hot shower, placing the spliff in the ashtray and letting it go out.

After about twenty minutes under the steaming shower, his bed called his name. Having stayed up for two days straight, he couldn't resist. He even denied Donna's persistent requests to spend the night with him just so he could get some rest. Wrapped up in a robe, Dolla strolled off into his bedroom, where he relit his spliff. Puffing away on his spliff, he decided to get himself a drink and check on Face and Bam at the same time.

Just as he got to the living room, he found Bam seated at the dining table, fork deep in some Chinese food. Opting not to interrupt, he walked straight to the refrigerator and grabbed himself a bottle of water.

"In the a.m." He said casually as he walked past Bam.

Acknowledging with a nod, Bam continued his feast. Dolla walked straight to the back of the house where he found Face by the backdoor, putting the finishing touches on a spliff. Face and Dolla made small talk, each of them puffing away on their own spliff. After a moment, Dolla felt the effects of the spliff so he decided to call it a night.

"I'll holla in the a.m." He said while bumping fists with Face before walking off to his bedroom. Once he arrived inside, he checked all his hiding spots where he had methodically placed guns. Satisfied, he finished his spliff while taking sips from the bottle of water. He now stared blankly at the flat screen television, contemplating their next move.

It didn't take Dolla long to fall asleep. Actually, he passed out with the television on.

Chapter 37: LAST DAYS

Darkness gradually loomed over the fall skies on the evening of KD's last night in New York. Tonight was the night he'd be leaving for his special vacation. An untimely but much needed vacation, possibly with no return. *No one knows what the future holds,* they say. But how does one explain this sudden change?

Is my life some kind of movie script, with edits at any possible moment? What bothers me most is the fact that I'm not the one making the edits. KD's thoughts ran rampant as he stared blankly out of the sliding glass doors leading to the patio.

This is the life I chose, the path I've travelled on, and well, tonight, I must continue my journey. He concluded to himself quietly.

Never let them see you sweat. His uncle Black had always said to him as he was growing up. Tonight, he was no longer that teenage boy, with his manhood put to the ultimate test as he faced this untimely challenge. Was he ready to part with everything and everybody in his life? Only he knew.

In a matter of hours, the place he called home for nearly three decades would become a mere blurry sight, as he traveled back to his roots. The place he had lived and loved his entire adult life, forging unbreakable relationships with some of the most beautiful and important individuals he'd ever encountered. How does one cope with such a major change? Bad enough most people think he'd been dead.

Sitting in the spacious living room of Black's house in Jersey, surrounded by custom-made furniture, expensive pieces of art and fancy electronics, he thought about what life would be like back across the ocean after such a lengthy absence. From the plush crème leather sofa where he sat, the balls of his heels sunk deep into the matching crème-colored carpet as he stared absentmindedly at a portrait of Bob Marley, the late great reggae legend. In this particular portrait, the legend appeared to be in deep thought, similar to the position KD found himself in now. This made him wonder just what was going through Mr. Marley's mind at that particular point in time.

The spliff he clutched between the middle and index fingers of his left hand burned freely; traces of smoke rose towards the spinning ceiling fan as he continued to stare at the portrait, reminiscing about his life here in New York. The life that would soon become his past, part of his history. He remembered all the fun times he shared with Dolla and Poundz, as well as the bad times. The near-death situations, especially the incident that prompted Black to draw the conclusion to let the wrong right itself.

Having jumped bail on a double-homicide, the authorities sought after him heavily. With Nine gunning hard for him for killing Dre, life wasn't all peaches. Hell, with Nine's healthy bounty, everybody was a possible threat to KD's life. Black's suggestion that KD take an overdue vacation until things blew over seemed reasonable. After all, he no longer existed to most people so why not confirm their suspicions?

Granted this was a smart idea, the fact that his *brothers,* like most people, thought he was dead did not appeal to him. In fact, it burned deeply inside him day in and out. Considering everything they had been through together, no one deserved to know he was alive more than Dolla and Poundz. For it was because of his *death* that Dolla and Poundz had been mercilessly warring with Nine over the last few months. Word on the streets was that they swore they wouldn't rest until Nine was dead and gone.

This bloodshed has got to stop! He said to himself as he finished his spliff and tossed the roach into the glass ashtray. As far as he could see, he was the key to this complicated puzzle — Nine wanted to kill him to avenge Dre's death, and Dolla and Poundz wanted Nine dead because they thought he orchestrated the incident that *killed* Black and him. Talk about a touchy situation.

I need to do something before someone else gets hurt, or worse, ends up dead.

With that thought in mind, he downed the glass of Hennessy he had been babysitting and slipped into his Timberland boots. Snatching his .45 from the coffee table, he tucked the gun into his waistline and without wasting another minute, headed out into the darkness. In the garage, he occupied the driver's seat of Black's Chrysler 300. He stashed the pistol under his seat before turning the engine over. As the engine purred quietly, he thought shortly about what he was doing.

Since the only way to stop the bloody war was by showing his brothers that he was still alive, he pressed the button to open the garage door and watched through the rearview mirror as the door retreated upward. Before the door could fully clear, he reversed out of the garage on his way to pay Dolla and Poundz a surprise visit.

The silence in the car was deafening as he maneuvered his way towards the George Washington Bridge. He made it to the bridge quickly and stayed the course into New York, driving at a normal speed to help collect his thoughts. Once in New York, he tuned the car's satellite radio to an R&B station, keeping the volume just above a whisper, thankful for light traffic.

Past the tollbooths with no hassle, he realized just a few blocks away from Dolla's house that he'd been driving longer than an hour. He continued to navigate his way through the back streets until he arrived at Dolla's address. To be on the safe side, he decided to drive around the neighborhood to get a feel for the area. Considering how secluded the neighborhood was, he found little activity as expected.

On his second go-around, he eased the 300 to the curbside up the street from Dolla's house. Cutting off the lights, he let the engine idle for a moment. He transferred his .45 to his waist and quickly scanned the street before killing the engine and making his exit. No sooner than his Timberlands made contact with the pavement, a burst of gunfire erupted from the direction of Dolla's house.

Caught completely off guard, he quickly ducked behind the car, removing his own pistol from his waistline. On his haunches, he scanned the street again, not a soul in sight.

The gunfire continued; an exchange from what sounded like three different guns. An obvious firefight in his *brother's* house drove his heart to beat as loud as an African drum. He waited during a moment of cease-fire, followed by two distinct shots, then a long silence. A lump formed in his throat. An ordeal lasting a minute or two felt like hours to him. He said a quick prayer, asking God to spare his *brothers'* lives.

Fueled by adrenaline, he snapped into action. After another quick scan of the street before advancing cautiously towards the front of Dolla's house, he could see the front door cracked open as he approached.

"This can't be good." he whispered over his loud heartbeats.

He crept up and cautiously entered the house, gun at the ready.

Bingo! Lifeless bodies lay sprawled on the floor just as he expected; two in the kitchen and a third in the living room.

He was overflowing with adrenaline by now. A quick examination of the bodies revealed two strangers and one familiar face. He saw broken glass and blood every step he took.

Where the fuck was Dolla and Poundz? He wondered.

He proceeded cautiously but effectively to check the rest of the house. As he stepped out of the kitchen area and into the hallway, he heard faint voices from down the hall. Although he was not making out exactly the conversation, he pinpointed two distinct voices. He advanced carefully in the direction of the voices, gun still at the ready. Halfway down the hall, he made out some of the words mentioned — something about *last words* or *last wishes*.

He continued to inch closer and closer until he was mere feet from a half-opened bedroom door. From this position, he didn't have a clear view of the room but he distinctly heard the conversation.

"You die tonight, muthafucka!" A male voice bellowed.

"Fuck you, pussy!" Spouted from another.

This second voice sounded like Dolla, which prompted KD to lean in closer for a better look. He leaned in just in time to see an unfamiliar man strike a kneeling Dolla in the back of the head with a pistol. Dolla screamed out in pain, holding his head, then followed with, "Eat a dick, Nine!"

"Nine?" KD whispered to himself.

He was so furious that he followed his anger, barging into the room with such quickness that neither man acknowledged his presence.

"Die, mutha..." Was the last thing he heard Nine say before he silenced him mid-sentence with a headshot from his .45.

Nine dropped next to Dolla with a loud thud. For emphasis, he pumped two more shots into Nine's back as he lay slump on the floor. Not a pretty sight. He took a moment to examine the rest of the room — no other threats. He considered checking the rest of the house but he also understood that time wasn't on his side.

No time for small talk, he heard the wailing of

sirens from afar. From around his neck, he removed his African necklace and placed it atop Nine's lifeless body. Without a word, he ran out of the room, leaving a still-kneeling Dolla in shock. He sprinted back to the 300, pistol still in hand. He quickly took the driver's seat, turned the engine over, and pulled off the curb, leaving a trail of black rubber on the asphalt.

Epilogue 1: DOLLA

Dolla woke up hours later to the sound of gunshots. Unsure if he was having a nightmare, he continued to lay there dazed until he heard movement approaching his bedroom. Instinctively, he quickly reached in the drawer of the nightstand for his pistol but he was a second too late.

"Draw and I'll blow yo fucking melon off!" A deep male voice barked as the bedroom door flew open.

Dolla contemplated drawing his pistol but he knew that the wrong move could be his last. Caught sleeping in nothing but his boxers, Dolla decided to play along with the intruder, in hopes that Face or Bam would come in and blow his head off.

"Hold yo hands where I can see them," commanded the intruder.

Dolla complied by raising both hands.

"Now get yo ass off that bed!"

Again Dolla complied, wondering where Bam and Face were.

"Man, what the fuck do you want?" Dolla asked in an attempt to figure out the intruder's intentions. He knew that chances were that the intruder wasn't there to rob him, yet he tried his luck.

In response, the intruder said, "Interlock yo fingers behind yo head."

Again, Dolla complied before asking, "You sure you got the right house?"

The intruder ignored Dolla's slight jab and continued with his commands. "Turn around!"

Dolla did as told and instantly felt like he had seen the devil himself. His heart dropped into his stomach, making him feel nauseous. His throat felt like a baseball had been lodged in there. Never in a million years did he think he would be facing Nine under these circumstances.

"Did I answer yo question?" Nine asked sarcastically, following with a sinister laugh. He then added, "Now turn around slowly and get on yo knees!"

Dolla hesitated, earning himself a deadly blow to his ribs.

"You got hearing problems, muthafucka?" Nine asked before adding, "Turn yo ass around and get on yo knees!"

Again, Dolla hesitated but looking down the barrel of Nine's Desert Eagle, he knew it was only a matter of time before his patience ran out so he complied. As he knelt down, hands interlocked behind his head, his enemy with a cocked pistol behind him ready to take his life, Dolla knew his end was near. With each breath, he prayed for the most high to accept his soul. He had done his fair share of wrongs and knew he'd pay for it one day, but never expected it so soon.

The volume on the television went lower behind him, and the only sound he could hear was his own loud breathing.

"Almighty Dolla, do you have any last words?" Nine asked sinisterly, placing the barrel of his gun to the back of Dolla's head.

The cold sensation from the barrel felt like torture as he allowed the anticipation to continue building. Finally, Dolla had enough. "Fuck you, pussy!" He blurted out as if he was making a difference.

This earned him a deadly blow to the head from the butt of Nine's pistol. The force from the blow sent Dolla crashing to the floor. The excruciating pain from his head told him Nine had drawn blood.

"Aahh!" Dolla cried out in pain but Nine didn't let up.

He stood over top of him, barking, "Get yo ass up!"

Yanking Dolla by his arm, Nine shoved him back to the floor in the kneeling position.

"Eat a dick, Nine!" Dolla finally shot back, bracing himself to face the unthinkable. As he felt his own blood seeping down the back of his neck and the coldness of the barrel of his enemy's pistol, he knew his life was over. His heart beat faster as he continued to pray silently.

"Die, mutha..." Nine said before a thunderous gunshot interrupted them.

Blood and brain matter splashed over Dolla, followed by a loud thud next to him. Two more thunderous shots rang out, sending Dolla into a state of shock and confusion.

His ears rang. *What the fuck just happened?* He wondered but he wouldn't dare turn around. He heard footsteps receding from the bedroom.

Wait, somebody is running. What the fuck? He also heard the sirens from afar. He knew then that he had to do something before he ended up behind bars. He was still a wanted man after all.

Turning his head nervously, he found Nine, well the rest of him, lying dead on the floor next to him. Two large holes were in his back and his head resembled an exploded melon. The necklace he saw atop Nine's deceased body sent him into a state of utter shock. He knew of one person from whom that necklace could have come. The

197

sirens grew louder and louder, snapping Dolla back to reality.

With quickness, he jumped to his feet, picked up the necklace from Nine's body and ran to his closet for some clothes. Donning a pair of grey Champion sweat suit and Nike Air Maxes in record time, he rushed out of the room.

"Face! Bam!" He called out as he ran into the living room. He found both of his shooters lying unresponsive with bullet holes in their bodies. There were other dead bodies as well.

Looking at his dead shooters and the overwhelming evidence that surrounded him, he decided to do some damage control. In the bedroom, living room, and kitchen, he set fire to the house. He then disconnected the gas line from the stove, letting the gas fill the atmosphere. He knew it was a matter of time before the house exploded so he intentionally set off the house alarm.

He snatched his keys off the hook and into the garage he went. Jumping in the Escalade, he started it up and waited impatiently for the garage door to retract upward. As he listened to the sirens grow louder and louder, he backed the truck out of the garage and was relieved to see no police or fire vehicles outside. Putting the pedal to the floor, he maneuvered the Escalade out of the area with no specific destination in mind.

At that point, putting as much distance between him and the house was all he wished for. His wishes were granted as he passed speeding squad cars and fire trucks heading in the direction of his once safe haven. Just when he thought about the fingerprints and other evidence he had left behind, a loud explosion from the direction of his safe house put his mind at ease.

Epilogue 2: FAREWELL

The time finally came for KD to make his exit from America. He was clearly not ready, nor willing to leave the land he'd spent most of his life. Neither was he ready to leave his brothers. How about Karen? It hit him hard that everything he loved was being ripped from him. Nine, his archenemy was dead; he'd made sure of that. Yet, Black insisted that he takes this vacation.

Was a vacation with no set return date even necessary at this point? How about the conditions in Africa? Hell, he'd been gone for decades. He knew no one there; neither did he remember anything, considering that he left at such a young age. Although Black assured him that he'd be well cared for, KD was reluctant as the hours drew nearer. As always, Black knew best, and he wouldn't dare question his uncle's judgements or decisions.

Seated on his bed in Black's house, he looked at his suitcases, both of them perfectly packed and ready to go. He was fully dressed and ready to go as well. He examined his new passport and other travel documents. He then picked up the wad of cash he'd be travelling with, five-thousand dollars in total.

Finally, he stood up and walked to the dresser. He stared for a moment at his reflection in the dresser mirror and said to himself...

TO BE CONTINUED...

A MESSAGE FROM THE AUTHOR

To My Readers:

I'd like to personally extend my sincere appreciation to you for reading. I hope you enjoyed it. While I love to write, you, the readers, are for whom I write. Without you, there is no me. With that said, I ask that you take a little time to give me some honest feedback by writing a review. Tell me anything that you liked or did not like and share any suggestions you'd like me to consider. Whether negative or positive, I embrace feedback as they help me better my craft and create better stories. Also, if you enjoyed the book, please feel free to share with family and friends. Once again, thank you for reading, I really appreciate it! Now turn the page and enjoy excerpts from my other projects.

Until next time,

PB

EXCERPT FROM:

THE HITMAN: A Short Story

(October 2013)

One: Politicking

The Killer sat in the driver seat of his dark blue Dodge Intrepid, his eyes glued to his high tech night goggles as he embarked on another night of work. If things go as planned tonight, he'd make Mayor Miller one happy character. As usual, he'd found himself a well-hidden spot, from where he could perform his duties efficiently without drawing attention to himself. Tonight was no different from any of the other nights, cold or hot, that he'd spent alone in this very same vehicle. The loneliness didn't bother him at all. As a matter of fact, he enjoyed it. *Helps him maintain his sanity*, he claimed. Being the detailed man he was he took pride in every aspect of his work.

Through his fancy goggles, he observed Eleanor and her lover who had been making out in the lover's BMW for nearly ten minutes. The black-on-black BMW coupe was parked in the driveway of one of Eleanor's wealthy lover's many houses in an upscale Queens neighborhood. He watched on angrily, fingering the small detonating device wedged between his legs. He was sick of Eleanor. He was dying to finish the assignment at that moment, to end the cheating right then but he knew the timing wasn't right.

Having been on this particular assignment for nearly four months, he was having fun, watching Eleanor sneak around. He just didn't understand how evil and cold-hearted some people could be. Playing the good wife in front of the mayor and for the public but sneaking in and out of cars with this blond-haired jerk-off, Eleanor thought she had it all figured out, but little did she know karma was on her tail, and in due time they were going to meet one another.

These two had made The Killer's assignment easier by doing very little to hide their affair, thereby threatening Mayor Miller's political career. If the mayor had sniffed out the lies in Eleanor's stories, so would the public eventually. With the re-election right around the corner, the opposition party could've easily made a big stink about the issue. It hadn't taken The Killer but two days of tailing Eleanor to figure out she had something fishy going on. From Eleanor driving from the Mayor's house to a parking garage in the city, where a car service would transport her to a hotel to meet her lover boy, it was more like a rehearsed routine.

Karma was slowly approaching and soon there will be no more cheating for Eleanor Miller. Mayor Miller will have his peace of mind, free from the heartache. Maybe he can focus more on running the city as opposed to worrying about which guy his wife is running around the city with. Knowing he holds Eleanor's fate in his hands and that her days on Earth were numbered made doing the assignment more exciting for The Killer.

Through his fancy goggles, The Killer watched on as the lovers exited the BMW and walked hand in hand to the front of the lover's house, oblivious to the C-4 he had perfectly attached to the BMW's undercarriage. Like some teenage lovebirds, they stopped at the front door to make out some more, making The Killer's stomach turn. Eleanor Miller was indeed one cold bitch, and she was going to pay for it in due time.

The Killer watched the two enter the lover's house and made a mental note of the time on his wristwatch. Had the circumstances been different, he'd have jotted down notes in his pocket notebook but he understood that turning on the interior light of his vehicle would draw unwanted attention to his position. His pocket notebook and ink pen remained right in his jacket pocket where he kept it, its contents gibberish to an average individual. The Killer understood the importance of covering one's tracks in his line of work.

The evidence he had gathered for the mayor three months ago when he took on the assignment, including those hurtful photographs, had turned what started as a simple eye job into a real assignment, and he couldn't wait to see the conniving bitch die. He had contemplated not taking the offer at first but the fact that he felt deeply for Mayor Miller had compelled him. Witnessing a grown man of Mayor Miller's stature in tears that faithful day had brought back some unwanted memories of his that lead to his sudden change of mind.

To The Killer, it was one thing for a wife to divorce her husband and take half of his net worth but it was a completely different ballgame if she decided to stick around and humiliate him. Eleanor could've easily divorced the mayor instead of putting him through such heartache, at such a crucial point in his career. The Killer's job was not to figure out who did what and for what reason but this assignment had quickly become one of great interest to him.

See, before taking up this line of work, The Killer was your average working citizen, earning a living as a construction worker. This was until he discovered that his lovely Gigi was nowhere near as innocent as she appeared on the outside. After returning home from work earlier than expected one evening, he'd found Gigi, his wife of nearly a decade in bed with another man. What had hurt him the most was that his cheating and manipulative wife was screwing around with another man in his bed, under his roof while he worked to pay the bills.

For Gigi's disloyalty and infidelity, The Killer had gone to great lengths to cause her and her lover severe physical pain. Talk about torture! After tying the two to separate chairs and gagging them to suppress their cries, not only had he practiced his slicing and dicing skills on their naked bodies but he'd also given them a gasoline bath.

Then there was the shocking episode with the car battery charger. The Killer wanted, or rather, he needed answers and he knew that the connectors of a car battery charger would do the trick. He'd squeezed the answers right out of them, using the best methods he knew. In the end, they found the poor guy's body in an alley, miles from the scene, with his severed penis in his mouth. As for Gigi, let's just say it wasn't pretty.

Following this incident, The Killer had quit his construction job, sold his house and everything he owned, and moved to a different state to start afresh. After settling into his new place, he'd embarked upon a new occupation — an unlicensed private eye. His services were simple initially — if you felt your spouse was cheating, for a prearranged fee, he'd tail your suspected spouse until he gathered enough evidence to clear up your suspicions.

Through an old pal of his who happened to reside in his new area, The Killer had quickly developed a solid clientele. Occasionally, he'd receive a request to engage in a violent act, which if agreed, the client would pay quadruple the fee. These requests had doubled gradually, then tripled and ultimately he'd accepted what he'd become. He abandoned the private eye duties and became a full-blown murder-for-hire, whose services were employed by any-body from individuals to criminal organizations.

Watching Eleanor cause the Mayor so much emo-tional pain disgusted the killer to his core, same as Gigi had done to him. This was the reason he'd decided to em-ploy this particular form of killing. *By the time I get done, the medical examiner's office will be identifying Eleanor and this blond-haired prick by what's left of their teeth,* The Killer swore to himself as he kept a constant eye on the front door of the house.

He waited patiently for the two cheaters to finish doing the forbidden deed, occasionally glancing at his wristwatch. He contemplated breaking into the house; maybe he'd catch them by surprise and finish the assign-ment quietly. What if he's spotted by a neighbor on his way to the house? He dismissed the thought knowing that could be bad news for him. Some moments later, a glance at his watch told him it'd been longer than an hour, and Eleanor and her lover would be coming out any minute. He knew this based on what he'd witnessed on previous stake-outs.

The Killer continued to keep a constant eye on the front door of the house. About twenty more minutes went by and finally the front door to the house opened. Eleanor stepped out onto the porch first, followed by her lover. A smile appeared on The Killer's face as he knew his moment was approaching. He continued to watch as the lovers hugged and fondled each other like the hour and a half they'd spent together inside hadn't been long enough.

You might as well enjoy each other for the last time. The Killer thought as he continued to watch the inseparable couple with evil eyes. When the couple started walking to the lover's BMW, The Killer fingered his detonator yet again. He wouldn't dare miss his opportunity to complete his assignment as planned. *She does have some long legs, oh and those melons. Too bad she's going to die.* He thought to himself.

When Eleanor's lover opened the passenger door for her, The Killer nearly lost it, but he knew he had to wait for his golden moment. Then he watched the lover walk to the driver side and take a seat behind the wheel. Perfect! The Killer was thinking when suddenly he saw the lover reach for Eleanor. The two kissed passionately, and that was the straw that broke the camel's back.

The Killer had seen enough. As soon as the BMW's engine came to life, boom! The vibration from the powerful explosion reverberated through The Killer's body inside his vehicle, as he observed a huge fireball where the BMW had once been. As he drove away from his handiwork, knowing he'd left no survivors, The Killer looked at the rising smoke and gave himself a pat on the back for another assignment well done. There was no need in reporting this to the mayor, for he was definitely going to see it on the news.

EXCERPT FROM:

THE SEXTAPE: A Dedication to the Ladies

(March 2014)

A Cougar and a Cub

"You're not the only one with tricks, I can teach you some too, Dre." Maria's words continued to ring in my head like a nursery rhyme. How could I have forgotten that sweet voice of hers, laced with her thick Spanish accent?

Never in a million years would I have envisioned rubbing shoulders with a female of her caliber, not in such friendly regard anyway. There wasn't anything wrong with her. Older females just weren't my preference. Typically, I liked my female friends younger, my ideal being up to three years my junior. Needless to say, I found Maria special in a lot of ways, and some would say life was too short to be living with preference restrictions.

Maria was the type of female referred to as a cougar in the dating world, and in this situation, I was her cub. A cougar was commonly and informally used in reference to an older female who sought a sexual relationship with a much younger man, and a cub was the cougar's much younger lover. Another commonly used name that would suit Maria in this situation was Sugar Mama. While many younger guys may object to dating older women, I suggested giving it a try; at least once in a lifetime. The experience was well worth it. In my opinion, dating a cougar should be a fantasy for every young man.

It had all started at our local gym one evening when Maria sought my assistance with some abdominal and leg exercises. Having acknowledged one another on previous occasions with a casual hi, it wasn't until that particular evening that we spoke more than two words to one another. *Women, right? Only get friendly with a man when they want or need something from him*, I thought while laughing to myself. I shrugged off the idiotic reasoning and decided to help the poor lady out.

Initially, it felt natural that I was able to lend a helping hand, but then it became awkward when I later observed that certified personal trainers were readily available to assist gym members. This had become quite the situation, especially since Maria hadn't struck me as the cheapskate type that would refuse to kick out that extra dollar towards better health. I made a mental note to inquire about her reason for not participating in the gym program one day.

I assisted Maria with her exercises that evening and a few evenings thereafter. Over time, we developed a routine. We'd meet up at the gym and do a quick twenty-minute warm up on the treadmills, after which we'd split up to perform our individual sets. We even scheduled our cardio and leg routines on the same days so as to spend the entire session together, exercising that is. This led to more interactions between the two of us during sessions and ultimately, a casual relationship outside of the gym.

Gradually, we learned more and more about one another, even exchanging phone numbers at one point. Over the course of about three months, I knew Maria was a Puerto Rican divorcee with one child, a boy who was off to college. I knew she was a successful dentist with her own practice, owned her home, which she shared with her cat, Ziggy. She loved to dance, mostly salsa and was a wine fanatic. I also knew she had very few friends and drove the latest Mercedes Benz SUV.

"You're not the only one with tricks; I can teach you some too, Dre." Maria had said to me one evening as we parted ways after a cardio session. That evening, I pondered her words as I stood under the shower in my apartment. What kind of tricks was she referring to? Was she suggesting something outside of the gym? And if so, what? I found it highly unlikely that she was referring to tricks inside the gym. Let's be honest here, what kind of tricks could she possibly teach me with regards to my routines? Don't get me wrong, I was always opened to suggestions, but actual tricks? I was definitely lost.

Nearly four months had gone by since the day

nothing more than a casual relationship outside of the gym. We scarcely spoke on the phone and our biggest highlight had been an unintentional meet up at a shopping plaza one afternoon. Even that encounter had been very brief, only lasting a few minutes. No complaints from my end because the reality was that I hadn't expected anything beyond that. As far as I was concerned, our relationship was built solely on a mutual interest in exercising, or more specifically, her need for help and my willingness to assist.

I must admit, though, I was the type of guy whose dating policy could be strict or flexible, depending on the woman and the circumstances. Call it weird if you so choose but my policy had proven to be quite effective over the years. If Maria was indeed suggesting that we spend more time outside of the gym, then I was willing to make an exception. Maria, although nearly old enough to be my mother, was very attractive. At forty-two and even with a child, she was very beautiful, with the body of a twenty-one year old. It was a no brainer how she maintained her body, considering that we'd met at the local gym.

That evening, I decided to give Maria a call to clear things up after my shower, for my own sake. I refused to walk around confused like a chicken with its head cut off, or better yet, embarrass myself all because I misinterpreted her words. I finished my shower, got dressed, and had some curry chicken and white rice I had picked up for dinner, at the neighborhood Caribbean deli. As I sat at the dining table, forkful into my dinner, I began to have second thoughts about calling Maria. *Was such a phone call really necessary? Why don't I just ask her the next time I see her?* I wondered.

I reasoned that communicating effectively would be key in this situation and that the worst that could happen was she'd tell me she meant nothing by her statement. At which point I may look like a fool and even feel a bit awkward the next time I saw her, but on the positive side, I'd at least know where I stood with her. I finished my dinner and mustered some courage to place the call.

"Hola, papi." Maria answered on the third ring, her voice as sweet as always in her native tongue.

"Hi, Maria, hope this isn't a bad time." I responded calmly. I didn't want to bother her if she actually had something important going on.

"Oh no, I'm not doing anything much. Just having some wine and watching a movie with Ziggy."

"Oh, cool. What're you guys watching?" I asked. I had to figure out a way to slip my question in without sounding creepy.

"About Last Night. Kevin Hart is one of my favorites." Again with that sweet innocent voice of hers.

I started to wonder why she hadn't settled down with anyone since her divorce. It had been nearly ten years, she told me. For the short period we had known one another, it had been Ziggy and I this, or Ziggy and I that. Did she prefer the lonely life? *Different strokes for different folks, right?* I reasoned.

"Oh yea, Kevin is one funny guy." I played along.

"How about you? What're you doing?" It was her turn to ask the questions.

"Just watching a Knicks game and talking to you." My response was quick. I had to gain control of the conversation and I had to do it fast. Without giving Maria a chance to come back, I asked, "How did you like our session today? I know we did a lot more than our usual so I wanted to check on you, see how you're feeling." There, my perfect excuse for calling.

"Oh, it was perfect! I loved it! I was actually gonna suggest keeping it at this level next week." Her response told me I had her undivided attention so I pressed on.

"Are you sure you'll be able to hang? Maybe you should wait and see how it feels tomorrow." I teased.

"I'm a big girl, I can handle it."

"Okay, if you say so. I have a few more tricks I can show you next week." I eased a hint in there to see if Maria would take the bait.

"So you think you're the only one with tricks? I can teach you some tricks too, y'know?" She took the bait!

Maria had no idea how happy I was on the other end of the phone. "Is that right?" I asked before adding, "You could lead next week's routine then if that's the case." Another bait. I needed to know what kind of tricks she was referring to.

"Oh baby, I know just what I'm doing, and trust me, we're not gonna need a gym for my tricks." Maria said to my surprise.

Her response nearly caused me to scream aloud. Baby? We're not gonna need a gym? What? Had she not made a similar comment in the gym earlier, I'd have definitely thought she'd had one glass too many. I had to explore this to my advantage.

"This gotta be the wine talking, Maria. Why don't I call you tomorrow so we can talk?" I kept fishing. I needed to make sure the conversation headed in the right direction.

"Oh baby, I'm too grown to be making those little girl mistakes. I tell you what, why don't you come over for dinner on Saturday?"

I knew at this point that my hearing was not deceiving me. "Wait a minute, Maria, what's..." I had started to ask but she cut me off in mid-sentence.

"What do you like steak? Chicken? Ribs? Pork chops? Come on over on Saturday, I'll make us something delicious. We'll eat, have some wine and talk more then.

Consider that my appreciation for all you've done for me these last few months."

A bit rude and dismissive, yet respectful. My perfect opportunity to hang out with Maria, in her home at that. She had taken complete control of the conversation, I had to recapture it, and I had to do it fast.

"That sounds quite generous of you, Maria. I'm very appreciative but I don't think this weekend is a good time. I may be headed out of town." I had no intentions of travelling but I had to keep fishing.

"Well if you change your mind, you know how to reach me." She sounded a bit unimpressed with my response.

"Okay I'll do just that but really, Maria, you shouldn't worry yourself. I helped you out of the kindness of my heart." Now I had control of the conversation. She was older than I but I was still the man here.

"You let me know on Friday if you'll be around or not." She was persistent and quite aggressive in her pursuit.

"Okay I will but like I said, you shouldn't worry yourself." I continued to play with her emotions.

"You let me worry about that."

"Okay, good night, Maria. It was nice talking to you."

"You too, baby, sleep tight." She had said before hanging up. I hung up on my end and took a moment to replay our conversation in my head. A simple inquiry had turned into a dinner date, and as for my inquiry, well, I had my answers. It was Wednesday so I had plenty of time to decide whether to have dinner with Maria or not. Thursday came and went, and on Friday, I met Maria at the gym for our scheduled routine. I watched her closely for any signs of embarrassment or guilt, or even anything out of the ordinary for that matter, but she displayed none.

Maria had been her regular self during the entire session. I equated her confidence with being comfortable with herself; I found this quite sexy. After our session, I assured Maria that I'll be joining her for dinner that Saturday and she wasted no time doodling her address on a piece of paper for me. We agreed on chicken and rice, or arroz con pollo, as it's called in Spanish. Maria was all smiles from the time I gave her my answer to the time we parted ways. It was obvious she was excited to host me.

Saturday rolled in gloriously, beautiful and sunny as predicted by meteorologists. I had cinnamon oatmeal and toast for breakfast and remained in the house relaxing most of the early part of the day. At noon, I did a little bit of cleaning around my apartment, nothing more than I do every weekend. I then showered and got ready for my four o'clock date with Maria. At about a quarter to three, I left my apartment dressed casually in a pair of jeans, sneakers and a t-shirt.

Retrieving my car from the garage a block away from my apartment building, I made a local floral shop my first stop. There, I picked up a dozen roses, half pink and half yellow. Nothing fancy, just the average friendship charm. From the floral shop, I drove to one of the biggest liquor stores I knew. Being that Maria was a wine fanatic, no better way to win her over than to show up with a bottle of good wine. I must admit, I'm not too big on wine so I had to consult with the store manager, who recommended a bottle of Russian River Valley chardonnay.

I left the liquor store eighty dollars lighter, thinking good God, this bottle had better done the trick. I called Maria to let her know I was on my way before setting off into the sunset for the fifteen-minute drive. *Perfect timing.* I thought after seeing 3:39 on the clock on my dashboard. I listened to some old school reggae on the radio during the short drive to Maria's house. I arrived in her neighborhood just before four o'clock, and judging by the nice houses I passed with their manicured lawns, it'd be safe to say that I was in a nice, quiet and most likely rich neighborhood.

I finally arrived at Maria's address and parked my BMW in the driveway of her beautifully painted single-story house. *That paint job must've ran her an arm and a leg.* I thought as I got out of my car. The lawns were manicured just like the other ones I'd passed on the way. There were security cameras and the light fixtures were beautifully designed. I remember thinking about how much it had cost to maintain a place like that.

226

I caught her peeking out of this massive window at me as I grabbed the bags from the backseat of my car. The front door was opened before I could make my way towards it. "Hola, papi!" She welcomed me at the door with a big hug before accepting the roses and chardonnay I had brought her. She was looking as stunning as ever in a blue evening dress that clung to her every curve. Her lipstick was bright red and highlighted her beautiful facial features. I guess it was times like these that she maintained her body for — to charm young men like myself. Maria looked absolutely beautiful!

I said hi and thanked her for inviting me to her home. "Ah, papi, you shouldn't have!" She exclaimed after smelling the roses. She gave me another hug and a peck on the cheek to show her appreciation. The sweet aroma of deliciousness invaded my senses as we entered the house. Before the front door was shut behind us, I thought, *if Maria's cooking tastes as good as it smells, then I'd make sure we have a second date.*

I removed my shoes out of respect and walked around in my socks. The foyer was spacious and beautifully decorated. Hell, so was the rest of the house for that matter. The floor was a glossy hardwood, clean enough to eat from. The furniture were custom-made, nothing I'd seen before. Everything about this house spelled expensive.

"Make yourself at home, papi. I'll put these in a

vase." Maria's words snapped me out of my daydream as I watched her strut off with the roses. When she returned a moment later, I was too busy admiring the elegant interior of her dining room.

"Would you like a drink? I'm having chardonnay." Maria offered.

"Sure, I'll take some of that." I replied.

Excellent choice at the liquor store. Note to self: Make sure to thank the store manager the next time you see him.

"The food is ready so we can eat now if you'd like. I don't like keeping people hungry." Maria said jokingly.

"No rush at all, Maria."

"C'mon, let me show you around the house then." Maria had said as she handed me a glass of chardonnay. Slowly we sipped wine and talked as we moved through the big house. With her Ziggy under her arm, Maria led me on an extensive tour. The furnishings and decorations spoke volumes. Elegant and tasteful would be a good way to sum it up.

After the tour, we sat at the dining table and refilled our wine glasses. I then helped Maria set the table by lighting the two candles she had perfectly placed on the table. Although I was a guest, I refused to play the part. Maria served us a mouth-watering chicken and rice dinner. Talk about deliciousness. In the dimly lit dining room, the candle light provided just enough illumination as we ate, talked, and drank wine. I was already making plans in my head for a second date. I've had this particular dish numerous times in the past but never this delicious, not that I could recall anyway.

After dinner, we sat around talking for heaven knows how long. We talked about anything and everything from traveling the world to the state of the world economy to our individual lives and goals. Maria was quite the conversationalist. The atmosphere had been pleasantly warm and fun since the moment I entered the house and I was planning to keep it that way. I was truly enjoying her company and hoped she was enjoying mine as well.

Finally, Maria decided to load the dishes into the dishwasher and I helped by scraping my plate and blowing out the candles. We then moved our mini party to her spacious living room with a second bottle of chardonnay. The leather sectional was super comfortable and the flat screen television, humongous. Maria surfed through channels for a movie and settled on Mr. and Mrs. Smith with Brad Pitt and Angelina Jolie. The movie looked as clear as water, the humongous television showing every single detail; with perfect surround sound which I deduced had been professionally installed.

About fifteen minutes into the movie, Maria excused herself to use the powder room. Upon her return, she closed the distance between us on the sofa. I didn't mind it but I couldn't help but notice it either. We were both adults after all. For the next hour and a half, we sipped wine and enjoyed the movie in silence with the exception of an occasional question from Maria; questions about parts of the movie she didn't understand. I answered her every question with as much detail and to the best of my ability. It was obvious Maria was enjoying my company from how giggly she'd become or maybe it was the wine.

When the movie ended, we both agreed it was decent enough, maybe a three or four out of five stars. The second bottle of wine was nearly empty and we're both feeling its effects. I started thinking that maybe I should get going, but neither of us was in a position to drive safely.

We were lounging around talking when suddenly Maria asked me a question that gave the word interesting a whole new meaning.

"Why is it that a good looking guy like you doesn't have a woman?" asked Maria.

No! Not that question. Any other question but that one. I thought to myself. "Well, Maria, if you must know, I'm single by choice." I gave Maria a short answer before asking, "Why haven't you settled down with anyone else since your divorce?"

Maria's answer was short and simple. "Because I have yet to find anybody worthy."

"Worthy in what sense?" I pressed on without giving her a chance to come back at me.

"See, about five years after my divorce, I went out with a few guys. I was willing to give it a second chance but it turned out that every single one of them was interested in what I can do for them as opposed to loving me for who I am." Maria explained.

"Hmm." I said. I was starting to feel bad for her. To avoid opening any old wounds, I limited my prying. "Well, I'm single because I've recently gone through two bad breakups and I've decided to give my heart a break." I offered a detailed version of my story, hoping to comfort Maria a bit.

She nodded in agreement and closed the short distance between us. We're now practically touching one another and could feel each other's breath. Maria then said slowly with a touch of seduction, "Well, I think it is about time you took your heart out of time out."

I simply looked at her, amazed by her response. I thought about saying something but before I could get a word out, Maria and I were mouth to mouth with one another. We kissed passionately for a few minutes, our hands combing through each other's hair. Her lips were soft and full and felt pretty damn good. When we finally separated, I didn't know what to make of the situation.

While I sat there surprised, Maria just flashed me her prettiest and most genuine smile. Another sure sign of confidence, a sign that she was comfortable with herself. There was nothing sexier than a woman who was comfortable with herself. This made me more attracted to her. We made eye contact and this time I was the one who initiated the kiss. Her full lips, just so inviting that I couldn't resist. We sat in Maria's living room making out until we were both breathless.

As I sat there, struggling to regain my breath, Maria placed her hand under my chin and lifted my head up. She then looked into my eyes and asked slowly, "Am I worthy of your heart?"

Her words caught me by surprise. I hadn't expected such a question from her. In response, I simply said, "Only time will tell, Maria."

She just gazed into my eyes and nodded in agreement. I thought I'd seen a spark in her eyes but I had no time to analyze. Maria leaned forward and still holding my chin up, took my lips in hers yet again. She reached around, placing her other hand on the back of my head and kissed me so slowly, so sensually. There was no point in holding back. I let my hands go on an expedition of their own, exploring Maria's firm and shapely body. She posed no signs of resistance and her dress provided for easy access.

With our lips together, I leaned Maria back slowly

until she was lying flat on her back. I broke from our kiss momentarily to reposition myself between her opened legs. Then I leaned forward and explored her cleavage with my lips. The sweet and fruity smell of her strawberry-scented body spray invaded my nostrils, heightening my desire for her. I kissed my way to her neck area, then to her left earlobe. Maria let out a soft moan, wrapping her arms around my neck. I worked my way back down to her cleavage with my lips.

Access to Maria's breasts was relatively easy since she was braless underneath her dress. I kissed her shoulders sensually and removed the spaghetti straps of her dress. I then pulled her dress down to reveal a pair of the most beautiful breasts I had ever seen. I sized them to be about 34D's, round and perky like that of a younger woman. Not too shabby for an old gal. I thought. Maria had the type of body that many younger women yearn for. Everything about her just seemed to be getting better by the minute. Maybe I'd give her the chance she was asking for.

First, I felt her perfect breasts in my hands, and then I massaged them gently. Nice and soft, it was hard to believe that she had a child in the past. Her nipples grew hard under my touch. I took that as a sign of arousal. From one to the other, I took Maria's penny-sized nipples into my mouth and sucked them gently, all the while lightly squeezing her breasts in my hands. Her moans were soft and sweet. Maria's hands roamed under my shirt as she rubbed my back encouragingly. I knew I was turning her on but I also knew I was turning myself on in the process.

I paused momentarily to catch my breath and that's when I felt Maria's lips on my neck. Gradually, she kissed her way to my ear and whispered, "Take me, I want you." Then she stuck her wet tongue deep inside my ear, giving me the chills. I freed myself from Maria, rose to my feet, and removed my t-shirt. She joined me in a flash, dropping her dress to the floor.

Maria's naked body was simply breathtaking. She stepped forward and kissed my lips, then worked her way to my neck and down to my chest. She reached down and massaged my manhood through my jeans, all the while kissing her way sexily down to my abdomen. I just tilted my head back and enjoyed the moment. Maria dropped down to her knees in front of me and unbuckled my belt. She then pulled my pants down to unveil my stiff manhood, which now stood perfectly at attention.

Without hesitation, she reached into my boxers and massaged me, her gentle touches causing me to hiss in excitement. Maria then dropped my boxers and took my manhood in her hand. She kissed the head teasingly while looking up at me seductively. I licked my lips at her, wishing she'd stop being a tease. Maria finally took me inside her mouth. Her mouth was warm, her soft lips delivering the best sensation ever. Maria sucked me skillfully, reaching between her legs to please herself with her free hand.

If I wasn't turned on by now, the sight of Maria

rubbing her cunt was enough to get me there. I watched Maria take my entire manhood deep into her throat, one hand on my bare ass while pleasing herself with the other. When I reached down and grabbed a handful of her long hair, Maria gripped my hip and moved me back and forth. I started moving my hips and for a moment, she just held her head still, allowing me to have my way with her. Talk about tricks, Maria sure had a few up her sleeve. They say experience came with age after all.

Looking down at Maria's naked body, her breasts bounced with our movements, her free hand busily worked in between her legs, it was impossible not to take her right there. I removed my manhood from her mouth and signaled for her to get up, which she obliged. I then guided her onto the sofa in the doggy position. I stepped behind her and examined her perfect ass by massaging and squeezing them. Her cheeks were nice and soft, just the way I had expected them to be. I gave each cheek a smack and Maria responded with a sexy, "Aye, papi."

I teased her fat cunt through her pink thongs, causing her to moan sweetly. Her pussy was perfectly manicured and her arousal was evident by the moisture from her thongs. It was time to go in for the goods. I pulled her thongs aside and teased her beautiful cunt, her sensitive clit as puffy as can be. Her response was sweet and encouraging. "Dame, papi." She sang in her native tongue.

I slipped my middle finger into Maria's wet cunt

and moved it in and out. Her wetness lubricated my finger to perfection. I added a second finger, causing Maria to moan louder.

She peered over her shoulder at me, giving me the naughtiest look. I increased the pace of my fingers and from the sounds she made and the way she gyrated her hips, I knew I was doing right by her. I removed my fingers and tasted Maria's wetness. She tasted excellent and I thought about going in for a lick but my dick was begging for some action from the way it throbbed. I inched closer and holding Maria's thongs aside, entered her. She felt warm and tight, the type of cunt that could make an inexperienced man cum fast.

It was obvious she hadn't had much male attention, not lately anyway. Or if she had, then she sure knew what she was doing. This is just what she needs, a nice hard dicking to make her feel young again. I thought. Gripping her wide hips, I pumped away at Maria's tight cunt. The sensation was simply phenomenal! It was obvious Maria was enjoying herself from the way she rolled her hips to meet my movements. I aimed to please. I delivered an unforgettable experience.

I'd been fucking Maria for about five minutes when I realized I wasn't wearing a rubber. I thought about pulling out but for what? If Maria had an STD then I was sure I had it too by now, and to avoid pregnancy, I'd just have to pull out. This was a mistake that I'd refused to make for as long as I could remember. What made Maria so special? What in the world was wrong with me? It was too late now but judging by how well maintained Maria was, I concluded I was safe with her. But these days one could never be too safe.

Maria's moans grew louder and louder as I continued to pound her tight cunt. "Aye, papi, you gonna make me cum." She sang repeatedly while looking over her shoulders at me. I did just that, bringing her to an orgasm with my long pumps. I never let up, nor gave her a chance to recoup. Her beautiful ass and hips were just too perfect in this position. I was like a jack rabbit on ecstasy, the way I was fucking Maria. I slowed my pace and reached around with my left hand to play with Maria's clit. Her sexy moans drove me wilder.

I pulled out of Maria and removed my pants and boxers from around my ankles. She wasted no time removing her cum-stained thongs and tossing them on the floor. It was time to explore different positions. I seated myself on the sectional and before I could even get comfortable, Maria was on top of me. She leaned down and kissed me momentarily while stroking my manhood in her hand. She then guided my manhood inside her tight cunt, elevating my desire for her. As she gyrated her hips slowly, I went to work on her perfect nipples, driving her wilder by sucking on them.

Maria's bouncing breasts and jiggling ass cheeks

were every man's dream. Back to the task at hand, I grabbed Maria by the hips and guided her movements up and down onto my manhood.

"Aye, papi!" She screamed out in excitement as she reached around and spanked herself.

I took that as my cue to help so while I guided her movements with one hand, I spanked her thick ass cheeks with my free hand. With each spank came her signature, "Aye, papi!" Maria's sweet voice only motivated me to give it to her harder.

The familiar rising of her moans told me another orgasm was on the horizon. I gripped her hips and pumped mine hard into her while sucking on her nipples.

"Dame, papi!" She screamed in pleasure, and I guided her hips perfectly to meet my pumps. "Mmm, papi, I'm cumming!" She sang sweetly and I continued to pound, bringing her to another orgasm. On top of me, Maria bounced up and down in sheer pleasure. I was feeling good and I knew she was feeling even better.

"Aye, papi." Maria cried when my manhood slipped out of her accidentally. She rose up off me and went to her knees on the floor. She then took me in her mouth again, sending me into a state of heightened pleasure. Maria manipulated my manhood in her mouth for a moment then stopped suddenly. She told me to lie on my back, which I obliged by lying longwise on the sofa. Maria climbed on top of me, facing away from me. I was confused momentarily until she adjusted herself.

Now we're in the famous sixty-nine position, her juicy ass in my face as she took my manhood in her soft hands. I felt awkward initially since I hadn't much experience in this position. I'd only experienced it once as a matter of fact. She took my manhood in her warm mouth and manipulated it skillfully like the seasoned vet that she was. "Shit!" I sighed in sheer pleasure. Her beautiful cunt and asshole staring down at me invitingly only rid me of any awkward feelings.

I lubricated my fingers with saliva and begun rubbing her tight asshole while sucking her cunt. Maria gave no argument so I took that as a sign that she was enjoying my touches. I continued to rub her tight asshole while licking and sucking her beautiful cunt. "Mmm." Her moans were muffled. Maria moved her hips in a circular motion, all the while pleasing me skillfully with her mouth.

"Put your finger in my butt." She stopped pleasing me momentarily and said, and I obliged with no argument. Maria was a true freak, my kind of woman. Classy on the outside, freaky on the inside. I thought.

I moved my middle finger in and out of her tight asshole as I sucked her pussy. Her excitement was obvious as she stopped pleasing me with her mouth momentarily to enjoy my touches. She moaned loudly, her soft hands gripping my manhood tighter and tighter as her glorious moment arrived. Her tasty juices flowed freely onto my tongue and I took my time, savoring every drop of it. I laid my head back down to refrain from straining my neck but continued to please her with my hands.

Maria returned to pleasing me and I enjoyed the warmth her full lips provided around my manhood. I was dying to feel her wetness so I ordered her to sit on me. She inched forward and assumed a riding position still facing away from me. This was the reverse cowgirl position I'd only had the opportunity to experience about three times in my life. I watched Maria make herself comfortable in this new position while stroking my manhood in her soft hands.

She slipped my manhood into her tight cunt, letting out a soft moan. With her back arched, she held on to my legs and bounced up and down my erect manhood. The moment was special and the sight, amazingly gorgeous. I reached up and grabbed her hips, and guided her movements slowly onto me. She threw her head back and called my name sweetly in pleasure. Maria was a true beauty, even for her age and naughty too if you asked me. Everything from her appearance to her personality was simply amazing.

Despite the gorgeous view and the excellent sensation, we hadn't spent too much time in this position. Maria decided to return to the original cowgirl position so I repositioned myself by sitting up.

She climbed back on top of my manhood and bounced up and down while making sexy faces at me. I smacked her ass and watched her ass cheeks jiggle as she bounced up and down. Suddenly, I got this sudden urge to fuck Maria in a standing position so I told her to hold on tight as I rose to my feet.

I found it amazing that my dick remained inside her. With her arms around my neck and her legs around my waist, I guided her movements up and down. My time spent in the gym, strengthening my back and legs was finally paying off. This was a great position and it was obvious Maria was enjoying it from the way she threw her head back in pleasure. Her moans were growing louder by the second.

"Make me cum, papi." She sang sweetly, repeatedly, and with slow and deep pumps, I gave her just what she asked for. She hugged me tightly while sucking on my neck as she climaxed.

I eased Maria back down onto her super comfortable sofa, our lips stuck together in a kiss. When she finally released me, I stood towering over her, stroking my erect manhood. She knew just what to do. She took me into her mouth once again and manipulated my manhood with skill. The sensation was blissfully amazing. I was ready to enter her tight cunt again and Maria had no qualms.

"You like?" Maria asked in the doggy position while smacking her beautiful ass and peering over her shoulder at me.

I just couldn't resist the lovely sight of her ass cheeks jiggling. From one to the other, I gave her ass cheeks a series of spankings, making her cry out in pleasure. I drove myself crazy in the process. Inching closer, I entered Maria while she peered over her shoulder at me seductively. I started with slower pumps, reaching around to play with her clit. Maria encouraged me with her sexy moans. She continued to peer over her shoulder at me, licking her lips and giving me the sexiest look I've seen on her face all night.

This gave me enough reason to pound away at her tight cunt. Gripping her wide hips, I delivered my hardest pumps. Maria's sweet moans turned into screams gradually, and the bouncing and jiggling of her perfect ass cheeks only motivated me. I was feeling good and was ready to bring myself to ejaculation. Then suddenly Maria reached around, and I thought for a second that maybe she wanted to tell me to take it easy with my pumps but to my dismay, she begun rubbing her asshole. She hissed and moaned in pleasure. Then I watched her lubricate her middle finger with saliva, stick it in her asshole and start moving it in and out. I had a perfect bird's eye view of the action. Maria was driving me wilder with her naughtiness.

I continued to pump that tight cunt of hers even harder as I watched her finger go in and out of her asshole. Maria was screaming with each pump. This was better than motivation! So much excitement, it hadn't taken long before I was ready to cum myself. "Aah fuck!" I groaned in pleasure as I felt my orgasm coming on. I thought about pulling out but with such a perfect view and so much excitement in the air, it was just too good an opportunity to pass up.

"I'm cuming, papi." I heard Maria scream out but I was too busy groaning to acknowledge her. "Aye, papi!" Were the last words I heard right before I released my warm load of goodness inside Maria's tight cunt. For a moment, I just slumped over her back as I struggled to regain my breath. I finally slumped onto the sofa next to Maria. She cuddled up to me, laying her head in my chest.

"I told you I can teach you some tricks!" Said Maria as she looked up and winked at me.

Tired and still fighting to regain my breath, I simply kissed her forehead and nodded my head in agreement. It was over and she had won. She had taught me her tricks just as she'd promised. Maybe it was time to consider making her my woman.

EXCERPT FROM:

LATOYA: A Novel (Unedited)

(Fall 2015)

Prologue

Latoya "Toya" Walker exited Rik's golden-brown Chevy and walked hurriedly across the street. She was about as excited as a drag queen at a wig convention. In her dusty black Reebok Classics, a pair of blue jeans and a black long- sleeved blouse, her five-foot frame moved with the speed of an Olympics gold medalist. Having just made some money off Rik, she was in a position to take care of herself for the day; or at least for a few hours. At this point in her life, only two things mattered to her — money and her fix, and not necessarily in that order. Truthfully, she only cared about her fix but the problem was that she couldn't have it without money or something valuable worth trading. She had been chasing this monkey on her back for nearly three years now and showed no sign of stopping or slowing down. It was a sad thing to see such a beautiful person destroy herself with drugs, but hey, who ever said life was fair?

She pulled her small welfare phone out of her rag-gedy purse, dialed her dealer's number and listened as she continued to walk hurriedly up the street. After getting the voicemail, she quickly hung up and redialed him. She was determined to get her fix, even if it meant showing up un-announced. Her excitement was beginning to fade the longer the phone rang. Luckily, she succeeded this time.

"Yo," answered Dolla, her heroine dealer.

"What's up, D? I need to see you!" She said quickly into the small *Obama-phone* as they called it in the hood.

"Who dis, T? Yo I ain't around," responded Dolla.

"C'mon, D! Please stop playing." She managed to blurt out. She hated when Dolla played games with her but she also knew it was all her fault.

"Yo T, I'm out in Harlem shopping." For the many times she'd called him with no money or simply with some useless junk to trade, Dolla had eventually grown tired of her.

"For real, D. I'm good!" Toya pleaded her case. She could've easily said screw Dolla and go spend her money elsewhere, maybe with Gutter. The only problem was that Dolla had the best dope in the hood when it came to bag size and quality. That was aside from the fact that he'd helped her from getting sick on numerous occasions.

"Yo T, don't play with me." Dolla shot back with a serious tone.

"I'm dead ass, D. Why do you always do this to me?" Toya knew the answer to her question; it was more about the fact that Dolla was young enough to be her son. Nonetheless, when it came to drugs, it was a game of demand and supply. She wanted good dope and so she had no other choice but to play along.

"Cool, come to the block," said Dolla from the other end.

"Okay, I'll see you in a few, baby." Toya was excited.

"How long you gon' be?" Asked Dolla.

"I'm around the corner." Toya quickly said in response.

With that, the two ended the conversation. Truth is, Toya was a few blocks away, and just wanted to keep Dolla on ice. Little did she know, Dolla was hip to the dope-fiend game.

Toya placed the phone back in her purse and made her way towards a nearby bodega. She needed to get herself a few loose cigarettes to calm her raging nerves. While she cursed herself for the things she went through with Rik, Toya was thankful for Rik and the benefits that he contributed to her cause. She reemerged from the corner store moments later with a lit Newport 100 and a bottle of cherry coke. Toya continued her trek up the street, puffing on the cigarette like her life depended on it. She couldn't wait to take care of her business so she could get out of the streets, for the time being at least. Her only hope was that Dolla would be on the block as he said he would be.

It took her a bit of time to cover the four-block distance to Dolla's block. Upon arrival, she was more than happy to find Dolla politicking with another young man in front of his building. "What's good, D?" She greeted as she approached.

"What's good, T?" Dolla responded before asking with a stern face, "Yo, you good?"

"Yea I'm good, D, you ready for me?" Toya shot back, letting her emotions show. She had no intentions of being there longer than necessary. She had endured hell to earn herself some money, and all she wanted was her drugs so she could be on her way.

"Wait in the lobby; I'll be there in a minute." Dolla shot back dismissively. He definitely didn't want Toya's raggedy ass interfering his conversation with Bam.

Toya did as instructed but with attitude. She should know the drill by now. The front door to the building was opened so she had no problem gaining access. She finished her cigarette in the lobby as she waited impatiently to get she needed the real deal. She needed that good-good in her system. She was relieved to see Dolla entering the building a few moments later. The nicotine had helped calm her nerves a bit but she needed her bags. After a series of exchange with him, the two disappeared down the left hallway and into the stairwell.

"Whatchu need, T?" Dolla asked once they were in the stairwell and out of earshot.

"Two buns," responded Toya as she fished a crispy hundred dollar bill out of her purse. She handed the bill to Dolla who held it up high to the light and inspected it momentarily for authenticity.

"Where the rest at, T?" Dolla wasted no time demanding the rest of the money.

"Let me owe you a dub, D. I gotta get cigarettes." Toya responded.

"Nah, T, I need all mine." Dolla wasn't having any of that. He'd become so hip to the dope-fiend game that he had a comeback for damn near every trick they tried on him.

"C'mon, D, you're acting like you ain't gon' see me again." Toya pleaded her case but Dolla shook his head to let her know he wasn't having it. She dug in her purse again for more money. "All I got is ten, D." She said, placing two crumpled five-dollar bills in Dolla's hand.

"Yo T, you owe me a dime. Don't call me unless you got it all." Dolla said after taking the money and stuffing it in the front left pocket of his jeans. He then dug in his ass-crack for the two bundles of dope and handed them to Toya.

"Thanks, D. I got you next time I see you." Toya said as she wrapped the dope in a small napkin and stuffed it in her bra. There was no need in inspecting them; the *Punisher* stamp on the bags told her everything she needed to know.

"Don't call me unless you got my money, T." Dolla said as he got ready to make his exit.

"You know I got you, D." Before Toya could even finish her sentence, Dolla was out of the stairwell. Toya didn't care, though. She had her stuff, and that was all that mattered to her. She gave Dolla a few moments before making her own exit from the stairwell. She followed the short hallway into the lobby and out of the building's front door. She looked around for Dolla to say bye but Dolla was nowhere to be found. *Oh well*, she thought as she made her way up the block with excitement. She had her fix and a little extra cash left to get whatever she needed for the day. She was in dope-fiend heaven! Her next stop was a pizzeria near her apartment to get herself a slice, then it was off to her apartment to do what she loves — to get high.

ORDER FORM

(Book=$14.99 + shipping & handling: $4.99 = total: $19.98)
Free shipping on ALL orders to correctional institutions.
Customer Service: 347-912-1323, gumpublising@gmail.com

Send me _____ copy(ies) of THE GENESIS. I've enclosed a
$_____ check/money order for my purchase. (Please al-
low 7-14 days for delivery)

Name:_____

Address:

_____

_____

Phone: _____

Shipping Information: Same as above: _____

Recipient's Name: _____

Address:

_____

_____

Please mail completed form with payment to:

Ground-Up Media
951 Hoe Avenue, 7G
Bronx, New York 10459

ORDER FORM

(Book=$14.99 + shipping & handling: $4.99 = total: $19.98)
Free shipping on ALL orders to correctional institutions.
Customer Service: 347-912-1323, gumpublising@gmail.com

Send me _____ copy(ies) of THE GENESIS. I've enclosed a
$_____ check/money order for my purchase. (Please al-
low 7-14 days for delivery)

Name:_____

Address:

_____

_____

Phone: _____

Shipping Information: Same as above: _____

Recipient's Name: _____

Address:

_____

_____

Please mail completed form with payment to:

Ground-Up Media
951 Hoe Avenue, 7G
Bronx, New York 10459

ORDER FORM

(Book=$14.99 + shipping & handling: $4.99 = total: $19.98)
Free shipping on ALL orders to correctional institutions.
Customer Service: 347-912-1323, gumpublising@gmail.com

Send me _____ copy(ies) of THE GENESIS. I've enclosed a
$_____ check/money order for my purchase. (Please allow 7-14 days for delivery)

Name:_____

Address:

_____

_____

Phone: _____

Shipping Information: Same as above: _____

Recipient's Name: _____

Address:

_____

_____

Please mail completed form with payment to:

Ground-Up Media
951 Hoe Avenue, 7G
Bronx, New York 10459

ABOUT THE AUTHOR

Peprah Boasiako is the author of THE HITMAN: A Short Story, and THE SEXTAPE: A Dedication to the Ladies. A veteran of the United States Army and native of the West-African nation of Ghana, Peprah currently attends college in New York City and writes fiction in his spare time. His upcoming projects include: Rebirth, Lost Cause, Feel My Pain and Ultimate Heist. Readers can learn more and connect with him at: www.peprahboasiako.com

Facebook: www.facebook.com/AuthorPBoasiako

Goodreads: www.goodreads.com/authorpeprahboasiako

Twitter: @NoReligionNYC

Instagram: @NoReligionNYC

CPSIA information can be obtained at www.ICGtesting.com
Printed in the USA
BVOW06s1927070815

PP6373700001B/1/P